Ambrosius: Last of the Romans

A Light in the Dark Ages, Part Two

By Tim Walker

Acknowledgement

My thanks go to my proofreader and copyeditor, Sinead Fitzgibbon (@sfitzgib), for an excellent job and much-valued guidance.

Also, I would like to thank my beta reader par excellence, Linda Oliver, for her honest and enthusiastic feedback.

Contents

Preface

The poor remnants of our nation... that they might not be brought to utter destruction, took arms under the conduct of Ambrosius Aurelianus, a modest man, who of all the Roman nation was then alone in the confusion of this troubled period by chance left alive.

Taken from *On the Ruin of Britain (De Excidio Britanniae)* by Gildas, c. AD550, translated by J.A. Giles

OUR STORY BEGINS in the year AD440 with the arrival in Britannia of young Roman tribune, Ambrosius Aurelianus. He is returning to the place where as a boy, then known as Aurelius, he grew up under the watchful eyes of an adoptive family in the town of Calleva Atrebatum. He is thrown into the politics of the time, as an uneasy peace holds sway over tribal chiefs who eye each other with suspicion, and are kept at heel by tyrant high king and self-proclaimed emperor, Vortigern.

This book is part two in a series, *A Light in the Dark Ages*. In part one, *Abandoned!,* a young Roman auxiliary cavalry officer, Marcus Aquilius, organised the defence of his town against a Saxon army led by Cerdric, a fierce warlord. This took place in the immediate aftermath of the Romans' withdrawal from their province of Britannia in the year AD410.

Sensing that the Romans would not be returning, Marcus chose to change his family name from his centurian father's 'Aquilius', to his Briton mother's 'Pendragon'. A new era of uncertainty awaited the Pendragon family - Marcus and wife Cordelia, their children, Uther and Esther, and adopted sons, Brian and Aurelius - as they looked to their defence from ruthless enemies, both within and without the traumatised island.

Place Names

Calleva Atrebatum – Silchester
Noviomagus – Chichester
Aqua Sulis (Caer Badon) – Bath
Londinium – London
Camulodnum - Colchester
Corinium – Cirencester
Caer Gloui/Glouvia – Gloucester
Portus Adurni – Portchester
Eboracum – York
Lindum – Lincoln
Deva – Chester
Hibernia - Ireland
Amorica – Brittany
Gaul – France
Britannia - Britain

Main Characters

Ambrosius Aurelianus
Marcus Pendragon (his adoptive father)
Cordelia Pendragon (his adoptive mother)
Tomos (his deputy commander)
Uther Pendragon (his adoptive brother)
Brian Pendragon (his adoptive brother)
Constans (his brother)
Germanicus – Bishop of Auxerre
Vortigern – High King of Britannia
Belinus – King of the Atrebates
Elafius – King of Dumnonia
Triphun – King of Dyfed
Brennus – King of Catwellauni
Hengist – Saxon Chief
Horsa – Saxon Chief

1. The Homecoming

THE WOODEN HULL of the royal galley of King Aldrien of Amorica cut through the choppy waters of the Gaulish Sea, passing white cliffs and inlets as the captain searched for a familiar landmark. Roman tribune, Aurelius Ambrosius, looked intently from the brow of his uncle's ship, searching for signs of movement on the shoreline, as the oarsmen guided it into the port of Noviomagus on Britannia's south coast. The cries of circling gulls echoed overhead, and a handful of startled fishermen eyed the fleet of fifteen ships with suspicion as they slipped, one by one, into the otherwise deserted natural harbour.

A fighting force of one thousand soldiers, half a cohort of Roman legionaries, half Amorican auxiliary from north-western Gaul, were ready for a fight, should they be met by any Saxons or hostile Britons holding the port. Aurelius breathed a sigh of relief at the lack of a reception party. His uncle's intelligence had proved to be accurate. They had sailed on the first favourable spring tide, after the gods had finally pacified the winter gales in answer to their offerings and supplications.

He sensed a presence by his side. "My lord, there is no sign of movement on the clifftops and a mere handful of villagers in the native settlement. The port is unguarded."

"That is good news, Tomos, and assures us of a pleasant return to our land." Aurelius shared a smile with his deputy, a native-born Briton, as were many of the auxiliaries who had volunteered to return to fight in their homeland.

"This port was well-chosen by the commanders of Emperor Claudius for the shelter it offers ships from the tempests without," Aurelius mused.

They glided to a halt beside the damaged wooden quay, which was devoid of life, except for a few curious boys, who marvelled at the sight of liveried slaves jumping out to secure the boats with rope. The boys gawped even more as two grey-cowled monks, with tonsured heads, climbed unsteadily onto the rotten pier. Horses and equipment soon followed, and an assembly point was established beside the stone ruins of the old Roman fortified port.

Following a victory over the Visigoths, in which Aurelius distinguished himself, Aetius, Roman legate and his general, had submitted to his nagging requests to return to Britannia. He was eager to assist his adoptive father, Marcus Pendragon, in organising Romano-British resistance to barbarian raiders. The Romans had abandoned their province of Britannia a generation before, but semblances of Roman-style administration and organisation remained.

Aurelius's grumpy commander promoted him from centurion to tribune and charged him with restoring Roman authority to the southern shore of the island. By doing so, he would be protecting his northern flank from pirates and more determined raiders. Aetius only agreed to send a small force, a cohort of four hundred and eighty battle-hardened legionaries and a dozen engineers, some of whom had connections to Britannia. A force just one-tenth the size of a Roman legion, but experienced in both construction and fighting, and more than capable of training a local army. It was a mission justified by Aetius as important for the purposes of intelligence gathering, but it was also a sop to a restless Aurelius, who had become a flea in his ear.

Aurelius was content with this; he got what he wanted. His royal uncle had added a further four hundred foot soldiers and one hundred mounted cavalry under the command of his brother, Constans, as well as ships and supplies. It was under

King Aldrien's roof, in the Roman-friendly kingdom of Amorica in north-western Gaul, that Constans had been born to Aurelius's mother, Justina, following her separation from her young son in the confusion that followed the sudden death of her husband, King Constantine. Aurelius had joined them when he had become a youth, following a childhood spent in the house of Marcus and Cordelia in Calleva. It was to there that he now returned. Once disembarked, he instructed the fleet to return to Gaul and took his position at the head of his small army, flanked by Constans and Tomos, with the two holy men behind.

They made ready to traverse a forty-mile stretch of neglected, stone-paved road from the coast to the half-remembered town his father, Constantine, had taken him to as a child - Calleva Atrebatum. It would be a homecoming of sorts, but with mixed feelings – his recollections of a happy childhood were marred by memories of the treacherous murder of his father soon after the southern Briton tribal leaders chose him as king.

"My lord, the men are ready," Tomos said, breaking his rueful reflection. "Surely we are taking the road to the north, my lord?" he added, seeing his commander staring wistfully down the road that ran west.

"Yes, Tomos, we go north, and shall camp in a clearing known to me some twenty miles on. You see me looking to the west, where once there stood a mighty and beautiful palace. It was built by the Emperor Claudius for a friendly local chief and is where my late father held court. I hear it is now a burnt-out ruin and, as such, lies fittingly with the bad memories of my childhood."

A white dust cloud indicated the approach of a dozen riders. From its center emerged the figure of a well-dressed noble on a magnificent white stallion. He reined in his mount and addressed Aurelius.

"I am Verica, Chief of the Regnii, in whose lands you have arrived. I see a Roman army led by a Roman officer, the like as has not been seen here since my father's time. Identify yourself."

Aurelius marvelled at the proud noble, wearing fine woven garments, a silver torque studded with jewels around his neck, and a thin golden crown restraining a mop of wild and wavy brown hair.

"I am Aurelius Ambrosius, Tribune of the Fourth Legion, leading this modest force you call an 'army' to Calleva, at my father's invitation."

"Then let us dismount and greet as men, for I have been expecting you," Verica replied with a smile. They clasped forearms and stood facing each other on the dusty track beneath a high rocky cliff.

"Hail Verica!" Aurelius said, matching his broad smile. "I am honoured to be received by you and your retainers. I see you have the bearing of proud ancestors after whom the Romans named this place. Will you ride with me a while? I wish to hear news of this island."

"I can do better than that, Tribune. We shall accompany you to Calleva for the council meeting of tribal chiefs. News of your coming has spread everywhere, and has prompted a gathering of chiefs and kings from the southern parts of this island. I have even heard that our king and emperor, Vortigern, will be in attendance. Come; let us start, as the sun is dipping to the west."

"You must call me Aurelius. We plan to camp this night at a mansio along the way, where we can talk some more." They mounted and the column moved out, climbing away from the rising hearth smoke of the crude coastal settlements, leaving the stone ruins of the port behind.

THERE WAS MUCH excitement in the former Roman garrison town of Calleva Atrebatum at the imminent arrival of one of their favourite sons, and a shared hope for the return to safe and prosperous times hung in the air. Senator Marcus Pendragon, now an old man in his sixtieth year, pushed himself up from his bed on a wooden staff, wincing in pain as he put weight on his swollen, blackened foot. His wife, Cordelia, and daughter, Esther, took his thin arms and slowly escorted him out to the courtyard of his villa, positioning him gently on a wood-carved throne between twin marble Corinthian columns, overlooking a pond around which children played. House slaves fussed around him, pouring thin, watered-down wine and offering platters of dried fruits.

Aurelius rode into the town through the south gate, over a wooden bridge spanning a dry moat, passing under a shower of rose petals to a rapturous welcome from the exuberant townsfolk. They were happy to put aside for a while their hard and edgy lives born of many years fighting off rival tribes and raiders. Aurelius had matured as a military leader and excelled in combat, and now returned as Rome's representative. He guided his black stallion, Perseus, towards the barrack enclosure, next to which stood the villa of the father who had adopted him as a forlorn orphan. He saw Marcus and his family standing in the shade of the colonnade outside their courtyard, laughing with delight at the sight of Roman soldiers once more marching onto their barracks' parade ground.

Aurelius jumped down and embraced Marcus, removing his purple-plumed helmet and tucking it under his arm.

"My father! I am much pleased to see you!"

"Ha ha! My son, Aurelius! You are most welcome, and your Roman legionaries!"

Aurelius brushed the dust from his epaulettes and shook his light brown curls, beating his chest in a mock-Roman salute, laughing happily at the assembled group. Marcus smiled with pride and the women gasped at his handsome features as his steady brown eyes moved along the line. Aurelius then embraced his adoptive mother, Cordelia, and sister, Esther.

"Mother, you look well and content, and my beautiful sister! I am most pleased to see my family again, but where are my brothers, Uther and Brian?"

"They will soon be with us. They are out patrolling our eastern borders," Marcus said, "as some homesteads have been raided by Saxons who have settled along the Ceint coast. They kill and burn, taking the children to sell as slaves. And how many fighting men have you brought to aid our cause?"

Aurelius took a step back and continued to bestow his radiant, confident smile on his family, warming their hearts, making them feel somehow more secure, as he looked around at their efforts to maintain their crumbling Roman way of life. He had been away for nearly twelve years, and was pleased to find his family and town still free and well defended.

"Father, I have with me close to a thousand fine soldiers, including mounted cavalry from Amorica under the command of my brother, Constans, six experienced centurions, each with an optio to keep the men in check, and a dozen engineers. May I present two eminent holy men who have accompanied me on my journey. They are bishops from Gaul. This is Germanicus and his companion, Lupus. They are sent by Rome to root out heresies amongst your Christians, but they can tell you more."

"You are most welcome and may stay here with us," said Marcus, turning to the holy men. "Please rest after your journey and we will talk more over our evening meal. My wife, Cordelia, will attend to you. She is a devout Christian and spends much of her time in our humble church, although I cannot vouch for her fashion of worship, as I still make homage to the old gods. That way, we are covered for divine protection!" As they departed, he turned again to Aurelius.

"My son, come with me, we have much to talk of."

"Hold, my father, for my brother Constans is coming from the barracks, and riders approach." Just then, a horseman rode through the gates of the villa, reining hard in a cloud of dust. They stopped and turned as a burly soldier in dusty armour, wearing an old dented Roman cavalry helmet, jumped from his horse.

"Uther! My dear brother and playmate! I can see you are now a strong man!" Aurelius clasped his forearm and hugged him. "How I've missed you and our sparring! We must talk tactics - I have brought many soldiers, and my brother, Constans, from Amorica. Here he is." Constans approached, shaking dust from his dark brown curls and wiping his almost black eyes with suntanned hands.

"My dear brothers, well met!" Uther grinned as he clasped forearms with Aurelius and Constans.

"This is a fine reunion, Aurelius," Uther said, "and I am pleased to finally meet your Amorican brother!"

"It is indeed a fine reunion," Marcus echoed, "but let us talk inside." He hobbled off, helped by a servant, along the colonnade in the direction of his study, once the office of the Roman garrison commander.

Aurelius followed with his two brothers, calling after his father, "And what of Brian, my fellow orphan?"

Marcus turned his head and spoke proudly. "Brian is now sub-commander to Uther, a fine soldier and leader of men he has proved to be. He is out patrolling and will join us later. He has married our daughter, Esther, so is now even closer to us. In many ways, I feel blessed by the gods to have three fine sons, although only one has sprung from my loins!" He beckoned

Uther to walk beside him, in what seemed to Aurelius to be a familiar arrangement. Uther fell into step next to his father, linking arms and chiding himself for his brief feeling of jealousy at his heroic older brother's return.

As they entered the study, Marcus was inquisitive. "My son, you left us as Aurelius, and return as Ambrosius, the Divine One, loved by the gods. This is a bold name to bear! How did you come by it?"

Aurelius laughed, "It was my legion name, as is the Roman way, given to me on my induction by a mischievous centurion who joked that my wavy curls reminded him of the likeness of Jupiter!"

"You may have to live up to it now, my son. I have a feeling that you have a great destiny in this island. The Council of Chiefs will convene here, in our senate building, tomorrow, and I will introduce you to them. You must be prepared to speak and give your reasons for coming."

Aurelius briefed them on the situation in Gaul and what was left of the squabbling Roman Empire. The Visigoths had sacked Rome and the empire had divided into two – east and west. His general, Aetius, was now an isolated figure in Gaul, fighting a desperate rearguard action against the Franks, dogged by treachery amongst his commanders. He paused and looked at the grim faces of the three men.

"We have had two emperors in the west this past year – Marcian and now Valentinian. Hail Valentinian!" Aurelius raised his goblet of mead in a mock salute, and the others laughed and joined in. They all knew it was a toast to days gone by.

"Come! Enough of Rome! I want to hear of your trials in the face of these damned raiders I hear about from my noble escort, Verica, who swarm like wasps across your land!"

Marcus shook his head sadly and would not be deflected. "Before we talk of our problems, let me say one thing. Your heavy words speak of troubled times for the once mighty empire of Rome, with emperors we have not heard of, put up by their legions. It is a portent of our impending doom at the hands of murderous barbarians who care nothing for our ordered and civilised ways. We are witnessing the end of our world."

"I can offer few words of consolation, my father," Aurelius solemnly intoned. "We fight against increasing numbers of people with no thought but for wanton destruction, rape and murder. They want only to destroy what is not theirs, and have nothing to offer in exchange except pain and death. It is a sad ending to all that Rome has built across these northern lands, although ruinous infighting and new taxes have also stoked up a dangerous brew." He cast his hand over a parchment map of the empire – the known world – tapping his finger on the triangular-shaped island in the top left corner.

"Here we sit, on this windswept rock, fighting against the forces of darkness, waiting to be overrun."

Uther scowled and muttered, "Not whilst we can fight back. We are not finished yet. There is opportunity in every situation, and your coming gives us hope, my brother."

"And not today!" Marcus roused himself as the four men clashed their copper goblets in a toast and drank again in defiance of their seemingly inevitable fate.

After a moment of reflection, Aurelius spoke in a quiet, measured voice. "What news of the villainous Vortigern, sly poisoner of my father?"

Marcus sighed, as he knew vengeance was on his son's mind. "Aurelius, it was never proven that Vortigern did the deed, although I accept he is the most likely culprit and had the most to gain..."

"Most likely! He took my father's crown! It was him, and I will make him pay!" Aurelius stood and crashed his goblet to the ground, sending it spinning to the corner, followed by a toga-clad servant running to retrieve it.

"He is now Emperor-King of Britannia, and is our overlord," Marcus said. "We must tread carefully and bide our time. That time may soon be upon us, my son, as he has set himself against the Council of Chiefs by hiring Saxon and Angle mercenaries to fight for him."

Aurelius sat forward intently, "This is news to me, my father, and a sure sign of his villainous nature."

After a short pause, Uther said, "Aye, there's growing discontent. He has already allowed Saxons to settle in the east, and they are even now creeping southwards and westwards, into our neighbouring kingdom of Ceint. From there they raid unchecked as far as our eastern borders, and we must mount regular patrols to defend our farmers..."

"Yes, yes," Marcus tersely interrupted. "We have fought off raiding parties from the south coast and bands of raiders from the east, since our victorious battle against Cerdric the Saxon many years ago. Our standing army remains small and we are forever on guard. But we are strong and determined, and fight under the dragon banner, uniting the people under our cause."

"Father, calm yourself," Aurelius said. "Your valiant deeds and slaying of Cerdric are spoken of far and wide, even in Amorica! You are the first hero of the Romano-British, but not the last. I am here to help, and more. Come, let us talk of our plans."

Uther eyed his brother and said, "Word of your coming has spread, and it will add some edge to our council meeting tomorrow. We must tread softly if we are to organise resistance..."

"Hush, my son," Marcus said. "Let us not talk of rebellion. Let me handle the murky waters of politics. One thing at a time. The chiefs must meet Aurelius and believe that he is indeed

'Ambrosius', an immortal warrior sent by the gods to lead us against our enemies. Vortigern will no doubt use threats to keep the kings and chiefs to heel. You can both concern yourselves with military matters in the morning. Uther and Brian are readying their men for a mock battle in the arena. You may find their methods and tactics of interest, Aurelius. Now, we must bathe and change, for your mother and sisters have prepared a feast!"

That evening they feasted in the Roman fashion, putting aside their political troubles over fresh oysters, roasted venison and the sharp wine of their own vines. When Brian joined them, Aurelius jumped to his feet and greeted him.

"Hail Brian! Well met! You and Esther were my brother and sister when I left, now I return to find you married to each other and I am an uncle!" he chortled, delighting in the strong relationships that had grown out of his own and Brian's suffering, in the loving household of Marcus and Cordelia. Uther was also with his wife, Jessica, and their baby daughter, Morgana. They were, for now, one big happy family under Marcus's roof. Aurelius was enjoying himself, his eyes wandering amongst the servants.

This had not escaped Cordelia's notice, and she moved next to him and whispered, "I can see you admiring our serving girl. Are you lonely for company, my son?"

Aurelius held her blue-eyed gaze and replied, "My dear mother, I was looking past her at that pretty youth. He is more to my taste."

She blushed and her eyes betrayed her disapproval. "This is not Rome, my son, and we are not in the habit of abusing our household slaves."

Aurelius squeezed her arm and said, "Then I will not offend you under your roof, dear mother."

The following morning the four brothers took their soldiers out of the town's walls to conduct tactical manoeuvres, whilst Marcus went to the senate to talk with the town elders and the slowly assembling chiefs from neighbouring lands. Cordelia escorted the two bishops, on their request, to meet the local priest, Father Andreus. As they approached, they saw him waiting for them, shifting nervously from foot to foot, outside the doors of his timber and thatch church.

"Nothing to worry about, my dear," Germanicus said, patting her arm. "We just want to find out if your priest is preaching the Augustine Roman doctrine and not the local variant we have heard rumours of."

2. The Council Meeting

A FALCON FLYING high overhead looked down rapaciously at the bustle of activity. The town was full to the rafters with visitors, enjoying the early spring sunshine and warmth that it brought. It was a chance to make money for lodgings in the old Roman mansio and the lodging houses and taverns that had sprung up around it on the south side of the walled town. On the eastern side, stables, workshops and warehouses were full, and to the north the pagan temples and a Christian church were a blur of ant-like worshippers. To the west, a procession of bright colours was leaving the former Roman governor's villa. It was now home to King Belinus, son of Valorian of the Atrebates tribe, who was escorting his uncle, Vortigern, Emperor of Britannia and overlord of all tribal chiefs and kings, to the senate building. The falcon wheeled over the empty space in the arena, looking for something smaller for its meal.

The assembled nobles rose to their feet as their emperor entered, trailing a red cloak with purple trim and ermine collar, and wearing a gold crown inlaid with sparkling jewels, taking his seat on a marble throne on a raised platform. He stood for a moment, stroking his reddish, greying beard, casting his cold black eyes over the assembled throng, standing tall and strong in defiance of his fifty years. The most senior kings and chiefs, numbering six, took their seats on wooden armchairs forming an inner circle around the senate floor. Behind them, on terraced marble benches, sat their wives, followers and minor chiefs. The room was full and stern warriors in leather tunics stood behind, lining the walls. Aurelius picked Verica out of the crowd and nodded.

Marcus, whose role was to make the introductions, sat close by his king. Aurelius sat on the far side of the room, close to the heavy doors, on a wooden chair, but not in the circle of kings. Vortigern summoned Marcus who huddled close between his king and his emperor. They had hardly met since the time of Vortigern's treachery to his brother, Valorian, when he sided with the Saxon warlord, Cerdric, at the battle of Calleva, in which Marcus distinguished himself as a young cavalry officer. That was almost forty years in the past, a past not spoken of, and Vortigern was now undisputed ruler of Britannia.

Vortigern spoke to Marcus in a whisper, "You shall introduce me first, as High King and Emperor of Britannia, and then my new wife, Rowena, daughter of Hengist of Saxony. Then introduce our host, my noble cousin, King Belinus, and the inner circle of kings, starting from my right and going around the floor, so as no one is deemed to be more important than others."

"Yes, my lord," Marcus replied. Vortigern continued to look keenly at the assembled group, packed into the building, settling his narrow gaze on Aurelius.

"Verily, there has never been a better attended council meeting. Perhaps it has something to do with the visit of our Roman tribune. We shall invite him to speak after the introductions so we can know his business on our windy island."

Marcus took to the floor, working his hands out of his tunic, and soon the chattering died down.

"My Honourable High King and Emperor of Britannia, Mighty Vortigern, we welcome you to our senate house in Calleva, home of King Belinus of the Atrebate people."

Vortigern bowed slightly in acknowledgement.

"And we welcome your new wife and companion, Queen Rowena, daughter of Hengist the Saxon chief, now residing on the Isle of Thanet." This last bit drew a glare of anger from Vortigern and a murmur from the crowd. Marcus moved on quickly.

"Our esteemed host, King Belinus, welcomes you, and invites you all to a feast this evening in our town square in honour of this visit from our emperor." This lightened the mood and drew cheers, banging on shields and claps of approval.

"Our council of chiefs and kings is assembled and I will now make the introductions. To my right, King Triphun of Dyfed, ruler over the lands to the far west and over the Demetae and Silures."

A large, round man with a bushy, red beard and matching ruddy complexion heaved himself to his feet and half bowed.

Aurelius's brow creased briefly in concern as Marcus coughed and then sipped from a goblet. Vortigern sighed. "I apologize, my lords," Marcus continued. "My wind is not what it was. Here is Brennus, King of the Catwellauni, our northern neighbours." A tall, elegant and expensively dressed man drew himself to his full height and nodded to his emperor.

"Next is King Elafius of Dumnonia, to our south and west, ruler over the Durotriges, Dobunni and Cornubia tribes and the fair Isle of Avalon. You are welcome, my lord." Elafius, a small man of neat appearance, inclined a respectful head to Vortigern, his fast-moving eyes scanning those around him.

Marcus turned and stepped to the centre of the marble floor, sweeping his right arm in a lavish gesture, and ignoring the pain in his feet. "Across the floor sits King Jago of the Coreltanui people, to our north and east." An unsmiling, well-built warrior, dark braided hair swaying as he stood, mimicked the nod of the others.

"To his left sits King Gorbonuc of the Trinovantes, eastern ruler and host to our noble emperor. You are most welcome, my lord." A stocky fighter stood briefly, shaking his chestnut curls, and managed an awkward half-smile as he bowed.

"These six kings, together with our emperor, will form our council." Marcus bent to Vortigern and then sat.

Vortigern pushed himself off his throne and stood, legs astride, his ringed fingers clasped in front of his flowing red and gold gown. "I welcome you all to our meeting, where matters of state will be discussed. But first, let me greet our esteemed visitor, Roman Tribune Aurelius Ambrosius. I was a mere youth when the last Roman legion left these shores, and since that time we have been left to our own defences and have restored our old tribal kingdoms. Pray tell us the nature of your mission, noble tribune, and why the empire of Rome has once again shown interest in us?" There were murmurs around the room, echoing off the flaking ceiling mural of the gods on Mount Olympus, now largely ignored. Vortigern took his seat.

Aurelius took to the floor, clutching his mace of office. He had taken Marcus's advice and forgone wearing the tribune's purple band of office over his red officer's cloak, so as not to antagonise Vortigern, who had claimed the sole right to wear that colour to denote his supreme authority in his kingdom. He was also mindful of his father's suggestion to speak in the native tongue.

"Noble Vortigern, High-King and Emperor of Britannia, I salute you and bring you greetings from my commander, General Aetius in Gaul, Legate of Rome, and representative of Emperor Valentinian." Aurelius bowed and thumped his chest in salute. All eyes were on him.

"My mission has no military purpose. I am here to visit my father, Senator Marcus Pendragon, who took me into his household as an orphaned boy, and saw to my early schooling in this town of Calleva. I sought the support and blessing of my general, who provided me with a personal escort of one cohort of soldiers for my protection. He is anxious for my report on how Britannia fares following the departure of Rome. He has charged me to advise you that we face a common enemy in barbarian hordes coming from the east, and therefore offers my help to you to organize your defences on your south coast against sea-borne invaders. He believes that his cause will be aided by securing his northern border and having an ally in this former province of Rome. Hail Vortigern, Emperor of Britannia!"

Vortigern had returned to his throne and was stroking his beard in contemplation of his reply. He stood once again, and Aurelius gave him the floor, retreating to his chair. "We thank you, noble Ambrosius, for your warm words, and welcome your offer of assistance to strengthen our defences. In truth, I am not sure that we need it." He paused here and preened, smoothing a sleeve.

"I have taken my own measures to improve our security by inviting our friends from Saxony and Juteland, across the Germanic Sea, to join our army. Together we will halt invasions of our northern lands from the Picts and Votadani. They will also help us fight pirates troubling our east and south coasts. Our western defences are in the charge of the noble Triphun, himself from Hibernia, of Scotti descent. Knowing the nature of these raiders, he is well placed to resist their incursions. So, you see, we have the matter well in hand." He smiled and invited the crowd to laugh and applaud him.

Having soaked up the love and loyalty of his supporters, Vortigern held his hands up for quiet. "You may assist us with military training as our commanders are eager to learn the latest methods employed by the Roman legions. To this end, I propose you meet with our kings and chiefs tomorrow in the afternoon, following our entertainment in the arena, and after we have feasted and toasted our success tonight in defending our own kingdom!"

Raucous shouts broke out, along with much banging of spears on shields and the floor, as Marcus guided the visitors and observers towards the doors, explaining that the council would now meet in closed session. He took Aurelius to one side and whispered, "Well done, my son; it was important to avoid confrontation with him. He has dismissed your offer of help, instead taking the opportunity to crow his own efforts, which are not universally welcomed, as you will find out. Enough politics for today, come and help me out of this place, I must check on preparations for the feast."

Minor nobles, knights and other supporters of the counsellors were spilling out of the building, jostling with beggars and hawkers in the bright sunshine. Marcus nodded to a few nobles and whispered to Aurelius, "There is a growing division between east and west in this kingdom, and your coming has sparked much interest among the western group who may come to seek you out, with a little suggestion from me, to be their champion." He winked mischievously at his son as he stepped gently down the worn and cracked steps of the senate building, supported by a servant, leaning briefly on the plinth of a statue of Jupiter.

He glanced at the temple next door, once dedicated to the god of Roman legionaries, Mithras, but now converted to a Celtic place of worship, a place he sometimes visited. He heard his wife call his name, and looked in the direction of the thatched, wood and daub Christian church further along the dusty road. He waited at the foot of the steps for Cordelia and the two visiting bishops to reach him.

"My husband!" Cordelia called. "We have celebrated holy mass and received a stern sermon from our esteemed visitor, Bishop Germanicus!" She took his arm and they moved slowly along the dusty road to their villa in the confines of the barracks. Germanicus felt obliged to qualify her statement.

"My lord Marcus, I was merely warning your Christian faithful about the dangers of heresy, particularly the teachings currently active in this land, brought here by Pelagius, known locally as Bishop Morgan. He is based close by in Caer Gwinntuic, and preaches against the doctrines of Saint Augustine and the Holy Church, confusing the faithful with his own wild ideas."

"Are you on a mission to stamp out this practice, Germanicus?" Marcus asked, somewhat mischievously, as he was more inclined to follow his mother's pagan Celtic beliefs.

"Indeed, my lord, our spiritual leader, John, the Bishop of Rome, has instructed me to come and offer guidance to our wayward brother. To this end, I have been advised to visit the Christian community at Caer Gwinntuic with my companion, Lupus."

"It is but a day's ride, to the south and west. King Elafius, their ruler, is here today, and I can introduce you to him at our feast this evening. He may allow you to return there with his retinue. Mind, I advise keeping quiet about rooting our heretics as he will not want you to bring discord to his kingdom!"

Germanicus smiled weakly, fully understanding the often-delicate relationship between politics and religious belief.

THE TOWN WAS a hive of industry and endeavour, as its traders seized the opportunity to make some money from their visitors. Roman coins had become scarce, but were still prized currency, along with pieces of silver and gold cut from bars and transacted to an agreed weight between buyer and seller. Brewers had been working around the clock to satisfy the demand for ale, brewed from barley and hops, and mead made from sweet honey. Brian showed Tomos around the six taverns that crowded each other near the south gate. They settled for the one recommended by Brian as having a reliable supply of tasty and less poisonous ales – The Wicker Man.

"Whilst the elders talk, we'll sup some ale," he said, clasping arms with a grinning innkeeper. "Brutus, let me introduce you to our noble centurion, Tomos, a fine Roman soldier with his forebears from this island of ours." The men greeted each other and Brutus brought them an earthenware jug of foaming ale with two clay beakers.

"Tomos speaks the Gaul version of our tongue, and wishes to tune his ear into our Brythonic language. I told him a tavern was the best place for that!"

"You are right there, Master Brian. I'll send you over my best girl, Regan, to teach him a thing or two!" The two men toasted their good health and slaked their thirst on the amber ale. After a short while an attractive girl, whom Tomos invited to sit, joined them.

"You're a pretty one, right enough," Brian said. "You're to teach my friend Tomos here to speak our language, and anything else you feel he should know!" The bar was full of soldiers spending their coin on drinking, whoring and gambling with dice, knowing that in a soldier's world time off must be enjoyed to the full, as seemingly endless days of stomping, training and fighting were the norm.

"How many soldiers do you have here?" Tomos asked.

Brian sent Regan off to organize a platter of bread and dried meat. "Best not discuss military matters in front of her or anyone not in uniform, just to be on the safe side. We have four hundred guards in barracks here, and I'm their commander. This town is a perfect square, with four gates facing north, south, east and west. My men are divided into four cents of a hundred, with each cent guarding one gate, manning one tower and patrolling their wall, in two shifts, covering day and night. In addition, we have a mounted militia for patrolling the outlying farms and our border posts, amounting to approximately one hundred men. Uther is their commander and they spend most of their time out there." He pointed to the south gate.

Tomos nodded and asked, "Have you had any trouble from invaders or bandits recently?"

"Only small bands of roving bandits," Brian replied. "Uther and his men have become skilled at slaying them. No large group or army has tried to attack the town directly since Marcus successfully organised the defences against Cerdric, when I was a boy. It was Marcus who found me, hiding in the forest after the Saxons killed my parents and burned our home. They have raided many times from the sea, testing our ability to oppose them, and we have sent aid to our cousins, the Regni, on numerous occasions, to repel them on the coast."

The two men took deep draughts of their ale, sighed in satisfaction and smacked the yeasty froth from their lips. Tomos asked, "So Marcus took you as his son, and then some time after, my lord Aurelius?"

Brian was staring at the blue sky, a faraway look in his eye. "Indeed, and Cordelia was a loving mother to us all. She was nursing the baby Uther at the time. Some two years after I was taken into their household, the brief reign of King Constantine ended abruptly with his sudden death, and his son, Aurelius, came to live with us. I was happy to have a new playmate of my age, and we lived and fought as brothers."

Tomos grinned. "I can see now how the wisdom and courage of Marcus has produced three fine soldiers!"

They clashed their pewter mugs in a toast and, after supping the fine ale, Brian resumed his report. "Our port town, Noviomagus, as you have seen, is in ruins after several sackings by raiders. Now the Roman fort is abandoned and the villagers there know to run to the clifftops when they see any sails approaching, as they no doubt did on your arrival. We also have

a plan to mobilize the farmers and villagers in a militia if
necessary, maybe up to an additional one thousand men."

Regan rejoined them with the much-welcomed food. As
they tucked in, Tomos duly applied himself to growing his
vocabulary and gathering some useful insights into life in the
crumbling town of Calleva. He could see the stone walls were in
need of repair where blocks had been removed. Brian told him it
was a problem that required guard patrols day and night to stop
the illegal trade in cut stone blocks and timber.

"A dozen men are in the cells, waiting to go before the
senate for trial. I or one of my officers usually gives evidence
and the guilty men are flogged, and if that doesn't mend their
ways..." He made a slicing motion over his own wrist to
illustrate the fate of repeat offenders. "In the old days, the
Romans would have crucified them, but now it is less easy for
tribal elders to mete out punishments of amputation, or impose
a death sentence, when feuding may be the result. Floggings
and fines are the most common punishments."

"You have become soft," Tomos replied. "Roman law is
much harsher, and many roads in Gaul are lined with the
crucified bodies of enemies, criminals and deserters."

"And what is your story, pretty Regan?" Brian asked the girl.

"My people are the Cantil, to the east of this place. Our lives
are ones of constant threat of killing or capture by invaders
from the sea or bandits from inland. My father's farm was
attacked and all were killed save for the children. We were sold
as slaves in the slave market and Brutus brought my brother,
Patch, here to work in this tavern with me. At least Brutus is a
kind man, and I am fortunate to be working here with my
brother, who serves inside."

Tomos was captivated by her and said, "I will pay Brutus for
you to be my companion whilst I am here, and no other man is

to touch you." She smiled dutifully, moving closer to him and holding his big calloused hands.

Brian laughed and ordered more ale. "Enjoy her company, my friend, for who knows where a soldier's road may lie!"

THE FEAST WAS a huge success, with the central square around an ornate fountain cordoned off to the townsfolk, who stood around gawping at the finery of the country's nobility. Cordelia was thanked by Belinus for the hospitality she and her ranks of women had prepared, and her husband smiled to see her praised by their king.

Marcus succeeded in keeping Aurelius away from Vortigern, who was happy to be flattered by his followers and the beautiful Rowena.

"Tomorrow morning there will be a mock battle in the arena to show Vortigern that our soldiers are ready to fight," he told him. "Brian and Uther will lead opposing forces with our training equipment – wooden swords and wicker shields. This should last no more than one hour, and I advise you to sit away from our emperor's gaze, perhaps with Verica and Constans, high up on the terrace. After that I expect Vortigern to leave, travelling with his close allies and neighbours, King Jago and King Gorbonuc. The remaining chiefs and kings will then meet with us to discuss matters pertaining to security and no doubt air their grievances about the Saxon foederati."

Aurelius studied Marcus's weather-beaten features and said, "I am happy to follow your wise advice, Father. It seems Vortigern is content to dismiss my mission as unimportant, which serves us well. Perhaps the other chiefs will see it in a different light. I am relieved that he made no mocking mention of my dear father, Constantine.

Marcus placed his hand on Aurelius's arm to interrupt him. "He has done you a service by not provoking your anger. Your time will come, Aurelius, just bide it and let me guide you."

Vortigern stood to indicate he was leaving. He swayed slightly and smiled in a drunken fashion, waving a hand to acknowledge the bows of his subjects, and was guided to a Roman litter, carried by four liveried slaves. The party soon broke up and quiet descended on the town as the fires and torches burned down. Aurelius and a servant took an arm each and guided Marcus back to his villa, merry with ale and ready for sleep.

3. The Games

BRIGHT MORNING SUNSHINE and the clatter of pots from the kitchen greeted the bleary-eyed Aurelius as he sent his youthful companion for water in which to bathe. Uther and Brian headed to the barracks to prepare their men for the mock battle. They had received instruction the night before that they must provide only one group of thirty warriors to fight against a similar number of Saxon warriors who were camped near the town. This was a new development, and they set about consolidating their best men into one group. Marcus asked Aurelius and Constans to accompany him to the arena.

Aurelius raised his hand to shield his eyes as he emerged from the arched entrance to the arena into the sandy pit. It was much smaller than the one he had been to in Gaul that seated over twenty thousand baying spectators in two oval tiers of arched stone walls. This one had a single tier circular stone wall, twice the height of a man, with one terrace surrounding a sunken floor that could probably hold no more than five thousand people.

Vortigern and his entourage occupied the commander's enclosed platform, and the terraces were filling with townsfolk eager to see a mock battle and find out if the rumours of wild animal baiting were true. There appeared to be no underground holding area, just an entrance and a high wooden gate at the rear. It was from behind this that Aurelius could hear the growls and grunts of animals, and he caught a pungent whiff of them on the morning breeze.

Marcus took his arm and guided him to a seated position high up the terrace behind Vortigern, where many of the kings and chiefs were gathering. They moved around the nobles, greeting them and making arrangements to meet later at Marcus's villa for refreshments before they set out on their journeys to their homes.

After half an hour, Vortigern rose to his feet to silence the crowd. "Dear friends, we gather today to witness our brave warriors fight a mock battle. One army wears the colours of my royal household, and they oppose Saxon warriors, who are not our enemies, but part of our foederati, fighting invaders from the north."

He milked the applause from the crowd for a minute, during which time he turned around and spied Aurelius. "We have not witnessed gladiators here for some time, save for the wretches captured in local skirmishes, forced to fight each other for the prize of life as a slave. I propose to our noble visitor, Tribune Ambrosius, that he puts up one of his Roman soldiers to fight my own champion, Sloane!" The crowd went wild, whooping and cheering at the prospect of blood being spilled.

"What say you, Ambrosius? Will you put up a champion?"

Aurelius rose to his feet and said, "Your Highness, you take me unawares, but I will take up your challenge and send my deputy to prepare a man."

The crowd was applauding enthusiastically as Aurelius signalled Tomos to come to him. After a brief discussion, Tomos said, "Sir, I have just the man. He is Ursulus, known as 'the Bear', and was twice the legion champion in wrestling. He is strong, but also quick, and will surely slay his opponent."

"Good, get him ready," Aurelius replied, "and ensure he knows it is a fight to the death."

Just then, two lines of soldiers jogged into the arena. One was led by Uther, followed by the slightly shorter figure of Brian; the Britons wore rounded helmets and carried oval shields of leather stretched over a wooden frame. The other line was of flaxen-haired Saxons wearing conical helmets and bearing round, iron-bossed wooden shields. For all the men, long wooden staves replaced spears, and wooden swords hung from their belts. The rules stated a warrior must retire from battle once his helmet had been knocked off. The two sides faced each other across the sandy arena, waiting for Vortigern's starting signal.

Vortigern stood and announced, "Let the battle commence!"

The two rows, each of thirty men, let out fierce warlike cries and lifted their shields in salute.

Aurelius leaned forward to see how the Saxons formed two rows of fifteen warriors, interlocking their shields to form a wall, protecting their front row from ankle to head. They advanced steadily on the unsure Britons, who responded to Uther's command and moved forward in a line, banging their staves on their shields, to meet them in the centre of the arena.

When the Britons got close, they yelled defiantly and threw themselves on the Saxon shield wall, trying to find gaps to thrust their staves through, or beat down on their helmets. This had little effect and they were driven backwards to the dismay of the locals. Uther and Brian seized their opportunity to attack from the sides, and rounded the wall, bashing the Saxons with staves and wooden swords.

"So Vortigern shows us the strength of the family he has married into," Aurelius said softly, leaning towards Marcus.

The older man looked at Hengist's daughter, Rowena. "And he can't grumble at the match."

His son's eyes narrowed. "What is his game?"

The Saxon's rear rank detached from the wall and faced up to the assault from both sides, and hand-to-hand combat broke out, with the crowd cheering whenever a warrior was overpowered and had to retire. Uther used his brute strength to knock the helmets off two Saxons, before coming face-to-face with their tall, powerful leader. His long, braided hair swayed as he swung his stave at Uther who parried the blow. Their struggle was mirrored by the smaller but swifter Brian on the other side of the melee, as he skilfully used his wooden sword to duel with two Saxons.

In the centre, Aurelius noticed, the front rank of the Saxon wall had achieved much success with overcoming the Britons, knocking them down with powerful thrusts of their shields and smashing their helmets off with their staves. Before long it looked a hopeless cause for the Britons, and soon Uther and Brian were surrounded and battered from all sides with wooden swords and staves. They would not give up and had to be knocked down. The crowd booed and jeered as the victorious Saxons held their shields and captured helmets aloft, shouting in triumph in their harsh Germanic tongue. Verica clenched his fists and howled his rage.

The two groups of warriors lined up in front of Vortigern, who held his hands up to quell the boisterous crowd.

"Our Saxon brothers have prevailed, and perhaps it is no surprise, as they are hardened warriors who have fought many battles and will greatly aid the defence of our island nation."

The crowd remained quiet and, after an awkward silence, Vortigern continued.

"Our motley Briton warriors have shamed us with their puny effort, and must be punished. They will now remain in the arena and fight against the wild animals we have waiting behind that gate." He pointed to his left, and all eyes looked with horrid fascination at the wooden gates at the far end of the arena.

King Belinus rose to his feet in protest. "My lord! Is it necessary to have our own warriors fight against wild animals? They are free men, not slaves!"

Vortigern turned his cold, cruel eyes on his host and said, "Dear cousin, they have failed to show they are capable of defending us from attack, and must now entertain us by fighting for their lives. Do not look so worried, they may have real weapons to give themselves a chance."

He rose to his feet again and announced, "To give the animals a fair fight, you must halve your force. Line up before us and my queen, Rowena, will select those who are to remain and fight. Now bring the weapons!"

The hushed crowd watched the young queen as she coolly released every alternate man, but left both Brian and Uther in the group to remain. She had seen how well they had fought against her Saxon guard. Uther laughed and rallied his soldiers with words of encouragement. Half were given swords and half spears, and they took the least damaged shields from their comrades, who wished them well. They stood in the centre of the arena in a circular formation behind their shields, waiting. The sound of cartwheels, the rank whiff of wild creatures, mixed with angry growls and howls, had set the crowd on edge.

Marcus stood and cried, "Not my sons! Are they to be fed to wild animals in front of us?" There was grim silence from the nobility as Aurelius tried to calm his father.

Four slaves sat on top of the wooden gates and slowly opened them with ropes. Two oxen, drawing a cage containing a pack of baying wolves, were whipped into the arena. Another cart followed, containing two angry bears. The drivers turned the carts, then unhooked the oxen and drove them out of the arena, barring the gates behind them. This left two large slatted cages, each with a slave on top. They looked up expectantly at Vortigern.

"My son!" shrieked a woman on the far side of the arena, and a nervous soldier looked up. Most of the youths were from

Calleva, and the only sounds from the crowd were uneasy
murmuring and the sobbing of their womenfolk.

The main arena gates were shut with an ominous thud as
Vortigern raised his hands to signal the release of the animals.
Each slave knocked out staves and lifted the rope-hinged side of
their cages. The crowd gasped at the size of the animals – two
hulking black bears, the like of which had not been seen in the
kingdom since Roman times, and twelve shaggy, grey, black and
brown-furred wolves, snapping and snarling. Their protruding
ribs showed that the creatures had been starved, and they
proceeded to circle the edgy soldiers.

"This is intolerable!" thundered Verica, as he jumped to his
feet, gripping his sword handle. Aurelius stayed his hand and
Constans implored him to sit. Vortigern turned around and
laughed, a cue for his queen and puppets Jago and Gorbonuc to
join in.

Eyes turned to the arena where a wolf was nipping at the
hind legs of a bear, which swung a paw and swiped its
tormentor off, yelping. Uther's voice could be heard ordering his
men to stand fast and wait. The other bear, shaking its huge
open-jawed head at the wolf pack behind it, lumbered towards
the flimsy shield wall before rearing up on its hind legs and
falling onto two terrified soldiers, knocking them to the ground.

This was the cue for all the animals to charge at the circle of
warriors, who thrust their spears and slashed at the animals
with their swords. A bitter and bloody fight broke out. Men
screamed as they were clawed or bitten by the ferocious and
hungry beasts. Uther advanced on the bigger of the two roaring
bears, jabbing at it with his spear as it reared up on its hind legs.

The crowd gasped and watched in horrid fascination as their
brothers, husbands and sons fought desperately against the wily
wolves, who attacked in units of three or four, selecting a target

and then rushing it. As an unlucky victim went down, other warriors took their chance to slash at the flanks of the wolves, wounding and enraging them. Their formation was abandoned as warriors grouped in twos or threes to take on an animal and slay it.

Marcus looked sickened by the scene before him that left the bloody entrails of his countrymen strewn about the arena. Aurelius studied Vortigern, who casually dropped grapes into his mouth as he pointed and laughed.

Uther and Brian each led a team of three warriors to take on the bears, wielding their swords and spears until they overcame the enraged animals and drove their weapons into the masses of black and bloodied fur. A huge cheer went up as the surviving group of eight warriors, scratched and bloodied, saluted the crowd. Both Brian and Uther were safe.

Scores of wide-eyed slaves hurried to remove the victims of the slaughter from the arena, before throwing dry sand over the bloodstains, giving the appearance that nothing had happened.

The entertainments were not yet over, despite a large portion of the crowd streaming out, and Belinus called forth the two gladiators to do battle. Two huge men stood shoulder to shoulder, their helmets under arm as they bowed to their king and emperor. Some of the crowd returned to their seats.

Vortigern stood and turned to Aurelius. "Noble Tribune, come here and watch with me."

It was a command not to be challenged, and Aurelius made his way to the royal box.

"Commence!" Vortigern shouted as he made a space next to him and invited Aurelius to sit.

The two evenly matched fighters paced around each other, probing with spear tips, being goaded by the few remaining spectators.

"My champion, Sloane, has killed many men in combat. What of your man?"

Aurelius stared out over the arena, watching the thrusts and slashes as the gladiators got the measure of each other. "My deputy has picked him from amongst the men. I do not know him, save for his reputation as a champion wrestler who has brought glory to his legion," he said.

"What say you to a little wager, Tribune? My sword against yours on our men. What say you? His black eyes gleamed with excitement.

Vortigern drew his long sword from its leather scabbard, and Aurelius marvelled at the elegant golden cross guard and round pommel, encrusted with jewels, and the shining steel blade glinting in the sunlight, bearing inscriptions in Celtic runes. Aurelius drew his gladius, its blade about half the length of Vortigern's sword. This drew laughs from the emperor's entourage.

"Nay, do not mock the sword of a Roman soldier that has slain many men in battle," admonished Vortigern. "My sword, Excalibur, was forged by a smith from a distant land, using the strongest and purest metals, with runic inscriptions said to protect the bearer. It is precious to me, but my faith in my champion is strong, and I would like to add your sword to my collection. What say you?"

Aurelius readily agreed, being not particularly attached to his sword. "It is a soldier's sword, my lord, and has served me well in battles against the Franks and Visigoths. I accept your wager."

The two combatants had thrown their javelins at each other without harm, and now squared up with swords, exchanging fearsome blows on their shields. They slashed, harried and probed, each trying to wear the other down and find an area of weakness or try to force a mistake.

Aurelius said, "You see, my lord, how my man probes with the tip of his short sword, looking for weaknesses, whilst your man slashes with his long sword, using brute strength. He may tire and make a blunder."

"Never!" thundered Vortigern, "He can fight all day long. He will win! Look!"

Ursulus staggered backwards as a huge swipe cut the corner off his already dented shield. Sloane grew in confidence and pressed on, swinging his sword at the fast-disappearing Roman shield. Ursulus dodged sideways and thrust forward with the full extension of his arm, nicking the giant Briton on his side and cutting one of the leather straps that held his chainmail in place. He cried in pained rage and continued his wild slashing. Ursulus dodged and weaved, and scored several cuts on his opponent's arms and body. Aurelius saw he was trying to cut away Sloane's chain mail vest, with sword thrusts aimed at the remaining leather lace holding the front and back pieces together. This was a gladiatorial tactic he had seen in the amphitheatre in southern Gaul.

Vortigern leaned in towards Aurelius and whispered, "I remember you as a boy, crying at your father's funeral. The noble Constantine, all too briefly King of Britannia. He served me well in uniting the nobles under one banner. Too bad he did not live to enjoy the power."

Aurelius stiffened, and he felt his hand moving towards his sword handle. Vortigern noticed and smiled, also gripping the handle of Excalibur. Aurelius glared at him with hatred, but said nothing, Marcus's warning, that his time would come, ringing in his ear.

A screech of pain was followed by sharp gasps from the crowd. The tension blinked. Both men dragged their gaze back to the duel, where Ursulus's shield was now reduced to little more than a patch of shredded leather over a crumpled iron frame, and he was bleeding from a wound on his bicep.

"Ha ha!" shouted Vortigern, "My man is winning!"

Both men were slowing as tiredness took its toll on their weary limbs. This aided Ursulus, who dropped to one knee to avoid a wide scything slash, the execution of which exposed Sloane's flank to the lunge that cut away the last remaining leather thong, causing his protective mail to hang to one side. The crowd gasped and Sloane looked down, allowing Ursulus to dart forward and drive his gladius into the soft flesh between his opponent's ribs.

With a look of surprise on his weathered face, Sloane stepped back, dropping his shield and clutching at the wound in his side, thick dark blood oozing between his fingers. Ursulus pressed home his advantage and hacked at his opponent's sword arm, cutting to the bone and causing him to drop his weapon. The big man staggered backwards as the crowd jumped to their feet, baying for blood. Ursulus hunted down his quarry, slashing and stabbing at the defenceless man, until at last he collapsed to his knees. The Roman legionary placed the tip of his sword under Sloane's chin and looked up at the royal box. All eyes were on Vortigern, who stared out over the arena in stunned silence. After a brief moment, he stood up and held his arm outstretched, turning his thumb down. Ursulus took hold of Sloane's thick greasy hair in one hand and, staring into his defeated opponent's expressionless green eyes, drove his sword into the man's throat.

SHORTLY AFTER, VORTIGERN and his entourage left
Calleva, riding north to join the old Roman road, the Portway,
to the east. He held his head high and seethed. He had refused
offers from Jago and Gorbonuc of their swords.

"I shall get my Excalibur back somehow from that Roman
upstart," he muttered to his wife between clenched teeth.

"Do not worry, my husband," Rowena said. "You must
summon him to your royal court and there we will see what can
happen."

The unhappy royal party made their way in silence, Saxon
guards marching impassively behind.

THE CLOISTERED COURTYARD in Marcus's villa was the
setting for a tense and gloomy meeting of the remaining chiefs
and kings, disturbed at what they had witnessed in the arena.
Dusty boots and sandals and scurrying slaves largely obscured
the tiled mosaic of Poseidon riding the waves, save for the eye of
a dolphin, at which Aurelius now stared. Marcus, sitting next to
him, interrupted his deep reflection by pulling at his toga,
craning his neck to see who was arriving. Uther and Brian,
having bathed their cuts and bruises and put on fresh garments,
appeared by his side.

"You fought well, my brothers," Aurelius said, standing to
pat them on the backs and offer them fruit from a dish.

"Aurelius! Come with me, my son. Our guests have arrived,"
Marcus shouted. They formed a line to greet the barrel-chested
Triphun, his huge frame wrapped in a red cloak, and his wife
Gweldyr, daughter of a former king of the Déisi in Demetia.
Their union had legitimised his conquest of what was now the
Kingdom of Dyfed in the far west of the rocky bulge in the

island. They were accompanied by Gweldyr's brother, Owain, Prince of Demetia, and Cadeyrn, Chief of the Silures.

"You are welcome, Triphun, our powerful friend in the west!" Marcus said, guiding his party to their seats.

Servants attended them as more chiefs arrived, filling beakers and offering sweet-scented delicacies. Marcus greeted them all and positioned them around the central fountain, on a raised terrace so that eye contact could be made above the soothing, splashing water. Round-bellied Belinus, King of the Atrebates, and his chiefs – Verica of the Regni and Drustan of the Belgae - sat with Marcus's family group.

Then there was the diminutive and watchful King Elafius, King of Dumnonia, accompanied by King Mark of Cornubia. Aurelius noticed how they glared at their neighbour, Drustan, as they walked past to take their seats. Finally, King Brennus, their northern neighbour, quietly took his seat near the entrance, shooting glances at those around the busy courtyard. Marcus spoke in a low voice to King Belinus, then stood and clapped his hands to gain everyone's attention.

"Noble kings, chiefs and invited guests, I am pleased to welcome you all to my villa as we share this special moment when our lands are in relative peace. However, we all know that outside forces are pressing in on us, and we must look to make strong alliances to safeguard our peace..."

"Aye, but we must also be wary of covetous glances at our lands from our neighbours," interrupted an unhappy Brennus.

Belinus shot him an angry glance and replied, "Our lands are separated by the Portway to the north, and there have been no incursions, Brennus, from our side. Please, Marcus, continue." Drustan and Mark glared at each other.

Marcus cleared his throat. "My lords, our main purpose is to further discuss our common alliance in the central and western parts of our island, over which you all rule, save for the lands between Brennus and Triphun, around the town of Caer Gloui, which is under Vortigern's rule. We can then hear from our visitor, Roman tribune and my adoptive son, Aurelius Ambrosius, whose natural father was King Constantine, our first king of Britannia. First, my lords, let us hear each king speak about the threats to his own land." He shot a glance at the sulking Brennus as he took his seat.

Belinus opened proceedings by speaking of the Saxon settlements in the south-east and east. He noted that Vortigern was based in the former Roman capital of Camulodunum, close by the port of Londinium and the Isle of Thanet, where the Saxon chief, Hengist, Vortigern's father-in-law, and Hengist's brother, Horsa, were camped with a swelling army. This was clearly a threat, Belinus complained, as both he and Verica were already defending their shores and eastern borders against Saxon raiding parties.

Verica spoke, confirming rumours that an army of Jutes had marched on Cantiacorum and now occupied the capital of Ceint, forcing King Corangon to submit to their rule. They had also occupied the Isle of Vectis to the south, and there were rumours that the Roman coastal forts were also occupied.

"They are under contract to Vortigern to fight the Picts and other raiders," Brennus said tersely.

"They are a threat to you all," Aurelius interjected, pushing himself up from his chair. "I have met the Saxons, Jutes and Franks in combat in northern Gaul, and know they are fierce fighters looking for new lands away from their salty marshes. They will eye your green fields and hills with envy, and take root in your land, spreading ever westward until you all are blighted. Vortigern does you no favours by inviting them in."

"Your talk is treason," Brennus hissed.

Belinus and Triphun, the two most powerful rulers, shot glances at each other, prompting Triphun to rouse his huge bulk from his wooden chair and take the floor.

"You know me as being of the Scotti people, from the western isle, now King of Dyfed. Yes, the Scotti continue to raid our coast, but also the south and west, and the Picts and Votadani come at us from the north. It is I who protect my lands, and I know my friend Elafius has also fended off raiders on his western shores."

Elafius nodded agreement.

Triphun continued, "The Saxons employed by Vortigern may clear his east coast of raiders, but they do nothing for us in the west, and I must agree with our esteemed Roman tribune. They will not return to their unproductive, oft-flooded lands. No, they will take root in the east and look to conquer and colonise us, one by one, kingdom by kingdom. Perhaps I have the least cause to worry, being furthest to the west, but I can foresee troubled times ahead for us all."

Brennus sneered in reply, "But you yourself, Triphun, are an invader from the very Scotti people our king has employed the Saxons to fight! Who are we to follow?"

Elafius took the floor, maintaining a short-stepped pace as he talked. "My lord Brennus, we have heard testimony from Verica that Saxons and Jutes are overrunning the kingdom of Ceint, and taking root along our south coast. We must combine our forces to resist them, for Vortigern and his allies, Jago and Gorbonuc, will not be able to control them."

Behind the inner circle of leaders, someone spat loudly at the mention of Vortigern's name. Aurelius stifled a smile.

The pacing stopped and the diminutive king faced Brennus. "We know that some thirty years ago, a Saxon army under Cerdric did land on our south coast and marched on this very town of Calleva, only to be stopped by the brave defences organised by Vortimer, noble father of King Belinus, and our host, Marcus. These are warnings, my lords, and we must heed them."

His words drew applause and shouts of support. As Marcus had anticipated, all were in agreement apart from the grumbling Brennus. He nodded to Aurelius to take the floor again.

"My lords," Aurelius began, "your high-king and emperor, Vortigern, did say at the council meeting that you may make use of my military knowledge. I propose that you all appoint me to organize your southern and eastern defences, against all comers, and to this end send as many fighting men as you can spare. They will be garrisoned and trained here, at Calleva, and deployed only in the event of attack. What say you?"

The kings and chiefs looked at each other and some whispered conversations broke out. Belinus took to his feet and quelled the noise. "My lords, we can work together to form this defence force and take advantage of the presence of a Roman tribune and his cohort. We must trust each other and make a pact here today not to invade each other's lands and to stand as one in the face of invasion. Who will agree? Say aye!"

There was a rousing chorus of "Aye!" and all eyes fell on Brennus, silent and downcast, with arms folded. "What say you, Brennus? Your lands go as far east as the Tamesis River, and may be the next visited by Saxons!"

He sat forward and slowly rose to his feet, standing in the light of a brazier that defied the dim shades of evening. "Mighty King Belinus, our fathers did squabble but were kept in check by the Romans, who marked the boundaries between our kingdoms. But I now see troubled times ahead. I am drawn to your proposal, yet also am wary of the wrath of Vortigern, who has a firm ally in my neighbour, King Jago. I must tread carefully, for I fear you would not help me should Vortigern and his allies sweep into my lands."

Belinus walked across the courtyard and awkwardly embraced his neighbour. "Your fight is my fight, brother Brennus. Let us make this pact, but keep it quiet from Vortigern, or his wrath may fall on us all."

4. Of Might and Miracles

BISHOPS GERMANICUS AND Lupus peered out from under their hoods through a steady grey drizzle as their horses trooped, heads down, behind a wagon, along a muddy track dividing a row of thatched roundhouses. They had reached Caer Gwinntuic, the capital of the Kingdom of Dementia, home to King Elafius. Round-helmeted guards holding long spears stood on either side of the gates to his longhouse enclosure as they passed through and were directed to the stables.

King Elafius paused as he entered the hall, his eyes slowly adjusting to the dim light. Smoke burnt his eyes and the stench of stale bodies made him gag.

"Get out everyone! This place smells like Hades! I want the side vents opened and this filthy straw removed!" He kicked at a clump of matted flooring as his minions were sent scuttling.

"Bring me my son!" he thundered as he strode to a raised platform at the far end of the long hall and took his seat.

Attendants fussed around him and his clerks brought parchments that needed his attention. Before long, a group of women entered from a doorway behind his throne, followed by four slaves carrying a litter on which sat a skinny boy. Elafius waved his attendants away and beckoned his son to come to him. The boy attempted to push himself up with thin arms, his spindly legs shaking as he tried to stand.

"Help him stand!" Elafius ordered, and his queen and her attendant each held an arm, preventing his crumpling to the ground. They guided him to his father who greeted his son awkwardly, with a gentle tap on the shoulders and kiss to the cheek, fearful of damaging him further.

"My son, it pains me to see you thus." He turned to the hovering attendants. "Is there no healer in my court who can help him?" he cried in dismay.

An ancient monk stepped out of the shadows, his white hair flowing beyond his shoulders, framing a pale, pock-marked face and his hands hidden in the sleeves of his habit. "Your Majesty, may I welcome you home," he said, bowing slightly. "I have been praying with your queen and your son, imploring God's mercy on his affliction. Your court healers have given him potions and bathed his distressed body, and we see a slight improvement in his condition."

Elafius cast the speaker, Bishop Morgan, a doubtful look and then spoke directly to his only son. "My child, Danius, are you feeling much better? Come and stand before me."

The boy, an only child, had barely survived ten summers, his precarious life a constant source of worry to his parents. "Greetings, Father, on your return. I-I can try to come to you..." He wobbled as he inserted a wooden crutch under one arm and made a slow, ungainly shuffle before his concerned father.

"That's it, my boy!" Elafius cried, in a cracking voice. "Go now and rest. We will talk later, for I must attend to urgent matters."

Danius was whisked away, and Elafius signalled for Morgan to approach. "Bishop Morgan, I do not doubt that your prayers are well meant, but the boy seems more pale and unsteady than ever. Where is my physician, Eppilus?"

An elderly man shuffled out of the gloom and stood next to Morgan.

"What say you, Eppilus?"

"My lord, your son remains weak and our efforts are keeping him alive but little more. We are at a loss to know how to cure what ails him..."

Elafius, spying his Roman visitors in the shadows, waved them forward. They and Morgan cautiously eyed each other and made slight nods of acknowledgement.

The fretful king was less concerned with introductions and made his frustration known. "Bishop Germanicus, holy man of Gaul, is there anything you can do for my poor crippled son?"

Germanicus bowed deeply and said, "Your Royal Majesty, I have seen the pitiful state of your son, and will add my prayers for his recovery. Is this a recent affliction or has he suffered since birth?"

"He was a healthy baby, but continued to crawl and cry long after he should have got to his feet. We know not what to do!"

"I do not profess to be a healer, my lord, but have seen similar cases on my travels. Perhaps you will permit me to examine him?"

Morgan cut in, "Your Majesty, I cannot see how this bishop can do more than we have already done to treat your son's condition..."

"Silence!" Elafius thundered. "The boy is getting weaker before my eyes! Your efforts are noted, but they have fallen short of a cure. I wish Germanicus to examine the boy and give me his opinion!" They scuttled away and Elafius turned his attentions to matters of state.

Germanicus rolled up his sleeves and washed his hands in water drawn from a well, and himself prepared a fresh broth of vegetables with a little meat for the child. This routine he repeated over many days and he insisted on taking Danius outside daily to feel the warmth of the sun and breathe the fresh air. He encouraged the boy to walk and build up the strength in his spindly legs.

Morgan hovered unhappily. Germanicus irritated him by using his Latin name, Pelagius, and he retaliated by refusing the

Roman bishop's request to preach a sermon to the Christian faithful of the town.

"I am their spiritual leader," Morgan stated, when pressed to give a reason for his opposition, before turning his shrunken frame towards his shabby hut, stepping around a trickle of scummy kitchen swill.

"And you have taught them to believe that man is born with free will to do good or bad as their nature dictates... and that is heresy!" Germanicus called after him, roused now to fulfill his mission. "You know well that our Holy Church in Rome has accepted the doctrine of the saintly Augustine, that man is born with original sin, and must therefore pray to God for absolution and forgiveness!"

Morgan retraced his weary steps and faced his accuser, attempting to straighten his back into a dignified stance.

"Your teachings have been condemned as heresy by the Councils of Carthage and Ephesus, and you must not continue to preach your ungodly ideas," said Germanicus.

Morgan shook his head. "I teach only that man's nature is good. We are all born with the same purities and moral ability as Adam, and therefore are free to choose a right or wrong path in life - and cannot excuse our own failings quite so readily by shifting the blame."

"We have all been tainted with the sin of Adam, original sin," insisted Germanicus. "That is the teaching of the Holy Church as sanctioned by our spiritual leader, the Bishop of Rome. We are not at liberty to make up our own beliefs! But I will bandy words with you no longer. Once I have healed the boy, I will have you run out of here!"

IT WAS AFTER several weeks away from court, dealing with disturbances in a far-flung corner of his kingdom, that Elafius listened with wonder and relief to his squire's report.

"The boy's condition has improved remarkably, to the extent that he now stands without the aid of a crutch and can walk a few paces. Germanicus has continued to feed him directly, with his own hand, a diet of fresh vegetables and fruits, fish, eggs and milk, and has brought colour to his cheeks by his insistence that your son rise from his cot and walk with the holy men as they pray."

Germanicus had kept both the court physician and Morgan away from Danius, having enlisted the full support of the boy's mother in this regard, and she had cried with joy to see her son's smiling face as he grew stronger. He now proposed that the child should be bathed, have his hair cut, and be clothed in a bright tunic and new leather shoes in readiness to greet his father.

Danius stood tall and held his head up, showing his father his clear eyes. As he thanked his father for the gift of a finely wrought buckle, speaking with confidence, it was clear for all to see that he was no longer a crippled boy, but a proud youth with the bearing of a prince.

Elafius wept with joy at the sight of his son and embraced him warmly. "My son! You are healed! Come forward, Germanicus, and receive my heartfelt thanks and praise for working a miracle!"

A murmur went around the hall at the word 'miracle'.

Germanicus bowed to the king. "Your Royal Majesty, I believe that if he follows the diet I have prescribed, and also my instructions on food preparation and exercise, with God's grace, Danius will grow to be a fine man and a royal prince!"

"Truly, Germanicus, you are a saintly man whose coming to my court has been a blessing from Almighty God! Furthermore, you have succeeded where others have failed." The king's eyes fell on Morgan and Eppilus.

Germanicus seized his moment. "Your Majesty, I am but God's humble servant, and through His grace have restored your son, Danius, to health and happiness. However, I must bring to your attention a serious matter of faith. I have found that Bishop Morgan is preaching a false form of Christianity to your subjects, spreading his own ideas that are at odds with the teachings of the Holy Church of Christ in Rome. He must desist from these practices, Your Majesty." The officious purse of the saintly man's lips then was in plain contrast to the open-mouthed dismay of his quarry.

Elafius narrowed his eyes as he beckoned Morgan and Eppilus to stand before him. "Eppilus, you have served my family well for many years, but it is now time for you to retire to your farm. I will seek to appoint a new court physician. Go!" The old man bowed his head, more in shame and sorrow than in courtesy, and shuffled out of the hall.

"As for you, Bishop Morgan, I have heard the rumours! That you demur on the subject of your ordination and you preach a feeble religious creed, one not stout enough for the Christian Church in Rome. Now that has been confirmed by Germanicus. But what is Rome to me?"

Germanicus bridled, and Morgan looked up; Elafius paid no heed.

"What most offends me, Bishop Morgan, is that, to gain favour, you have misled me, the king who sheltered your sorry bones, on your ability to heal my boy. He might have died under your care!" He glared at the startled priest.

"But Your Majesty, I acted in good faith and reject the claims of heresy, for I have simply found my own truth in the teachings of Christ..." The holy man's shock of white hair trembled, but his voice was firm.

"Enough!" shouted Elafius. "No more silver-tongued words, Morgan. Be gone from my court and my lands!"

Morgan glowered at Germanicus and said, between gritted teeth, "I will take my followers to the court of the Emperor Vortigern, in Camulodnum, where I will be accorded a better welcome."

"Be gone before I have you whipped," Elafius thundered, "and do not threaten us with the emperor!"

Germanicus bowed deeply as Morgan departed. "My lord, I will remove myself to the Christian church and begin arrangements for a festival in honour of your son's miraculous recovery. Good day, my liege."

AT CALLEVA, PREPARATIONS were not of the festive kind. Ragtag bands of Briton warriors arrived over a period of several weeks and were housed in the refurbished barrack blocks. There had once been accommodation for an entire Roman legion – up to five thousand men – and buildings were restored as carpenters worked around the clock to make roof beams, beds and furniture. Thatchers came in to repair the roofs, and cooks organised food stores.

Aurelius was under pressure from Uther and Brian to compromise on the strict Roman legion training and tactics.

"Our men cannot be told to forget all they have learned to take up the short sword and Roman shield," Uther growled at his brother one day. The three men had spent the morning undertaking their respective inspections and calculations in the town and had met together at Marcus's villa.

Before a visibly annoyed Aurelius could reply, Brian jumped in. "My brother, I feel a middle way is needed, as we may face forces of both Britons and Saxons, and therefore must be flexible in our approach."

Aurelius considered this. "On the field of battle, we can only fight in one manner, and a Roman shield wall will be needed to confront a Saxon shield wall. If there is some room for compromise, then let it be in the cavalry, with mounted archers and riders carrying small rounded shields, lances and long swords, in the Briton fashion. The Briton long swords are similar to our Roman cavalry spathas, although ours are slightly curved, to aid swift unsheathing, with one sharp edge for slashing and sharp point for thrusting."

Uther walked restlessly to the window and adjusted a wooden shutter against the late summer sun. Brian winked at him slyly and then turned back to his illustrious brother, his face diplomatically set in an expression that had never before heard of a spatha.

Aurelius had reached the terms of his command. "But I must be firm on legionary tactics when two armies face each other. The Roman way has been proven over hundreds of years to be the most effective. I shall command the infantry, Uther the heavy cavalry, and Brian the mounted archers. Is that acceptable?" Nods from both settled the matter.

"Brother Uther," Aurelius continued, "what is your report on the arrival of warriors?"

Uther cleared his throat. "We have had close to three thousand arrivals over the past month, since the council of kings, with eight hundred mounted warriors from King Triphun – some are Silurians and skilled riders, others wild men from the far west. Then there are groups of warriors who have arrived on foot, seven hundred from King Elafius and barely three hundred from King Brennus. Closer to us, we have eight hundred from our King Belinus, made up of Atrebates, Regnii and Belgae. Then there are assorted wanderers, looking for coin and a cause, some from as far as Gaul and beyond. Our biggest challenge is to overcome their tribal differences and forge them into one army."

"Then we must separate them into fighting forces under we three commanders," Aurelius said, his mind fully focused on military matters. "We must blend in my Roman legionaries and Amorican cavalry. There will be friction, but we must identify sub-commanders who can keep order amongst the men. Written orders will be in Latin, which all commanders must learn. Spoken orders will be in the local Brythonic tongue, which my Roman and Amorican soldiers must learn. We need two thousand Roman shields made, and weapons forged. And we have to fell enough timber to build ballistae and catapults, under the direction of my engineers. There is much to do, my brothers, and after a few days I wish to ride out and survey the south shore defensive forts. Let us make haste."

Aurelius had naturally assumed the role of commander. There was a mood of optimism that infected the whole town and surrounding area, as tradesmen flocked to Calleva looking for work. He withdrew to Marcus's study and polished the blade of Excalibur, admiring the long, straight, double-edged sword, and pondering the runic inscriptions in an ancient language he could not read.

This was where Marcus found him. "My son, it is a truly wondrous sword, fit for a king!"

"But I am no one's king," Aurelius glumly replied.

"You shall be, once Vortigern is deposed and you reclaim your father's legacy! I have taken the liberty of ordering you a fresh chain mail suit and leather breeches and wondered if you will ride beneath the dragon banner of the Pendragon family?"

Aurelius paused to think. "I had assumed I would ride beneath the banner of my legion, although I can see that I must appeal to the Britons if they are to follow me."

"Precisely! You should have a Roman standard and a Briton standard," Marcus declared. And what would be more appropriate than my own, under which your brothers have valiantly defended our town? The dragon is a powerful beast, a symbol of strength and guile. It is a commonly held belief that dragons still live in the mountains of Dyfed, far to the west, and sometimes fly across the sky in a trail of smoke and fire!"

"I will, as ever, follow your sound advice, my father. Indeed, I feel that you are somehow managing this whole situation; that perhaps you are a soothsayer and foreteller of future happenings." They both laughed.

"My dear departed mother, Morcant, had the gift of visions, and may have had some influence on me," Marcus mused lightly. Then he resumed the earnest tone of their planning. "Good, we are agreed. Then I will make you a shield design that combines the dragon and bear, the symbols of your Briton heritage and your Roman legion. These two creatures shall form your royal coat of arms, for you are a king's son, a royal prince, and you must now act like one."

"Then I have two banners, as I have also pledged allegiance to Rome and have the rank of tribune."

Marcus put his arm across his broad shoulders. "What you have is a powerful destiny. Rome has trained you to be a military commander so you can reclaim what is yours by right. You can be both tribune and prince, and Rome will thank you for pacifying these islands."

"Perhaps, but should I succeed, then it will eye Britannia once more as a juicy province, ripe for plucking with fresh taxes."

"You will deal with that when the time comes, and from a position of considerable power. The Gaulish Sea is a strong deterrent. Remember, it took Gaius Julius Caesar several years to land a successful invasion force, and the rebel Carausius held out for ten years against the might of Rome. Furthermore, I fear we are witnessing the final days of Rome's mighty empire. It is too weak and divided to bother you, and has already left these shores willingly."

LEAVES WERE FALLING from the trees, signalling the end of summer, as Aurelius and Verica rode out from Calleva at the head of a mixed cavalry unit of one hundred Amoricans and one hundred Britons. Aurelius had delegated command of the infantry to Constans, with Tomos as his deputy. Their intent was to sweep along the south coast, checking who occupied the fortresses and assessing their general state. The chances were that they would run into Jutes who now inhabited the large Isle of Vectis, and who had been raiding at will along the troubled coastline.

They arrived at Verica's encampment before sunset, and Aurelius requested a visit to the site of the former palace of the kings of the Regnii, where he had once run along the colonnade and climbed into a fountain as a small boy.

"I hope to have some memory return to me of the dim figures of my parents for, in truth, I cannot remember their faces," he said to Verica as they rode to the abandoned site close by the fortified Regnii village.

Aurelius dismounted and, accompanied by his patient guide, walked on what was once a path, through a rectangular garden, to a smashed fountain. Some building walls remained, but much of the stone had been looted, the encroaching dark trees crowding in from all sides. "I ran here, as a babe, barely three years old, towards the flowing waters of this fountain. If only I could form a picture of my mother's face..."

"Hold! Someone is there!" Verica drew his sword and moved towards the shadows.

Aurelius followed cautiously, moving between stone blocks and flakes of plaster, crunching mortar under his sandal on a part-hidden tiled mosaic floor. He was aware that they were without escort, his weapon also drawn. As they reached the steps to the colonnade, a figure rushed out from the shadows and with a cry slashed his sword down on Verica, who parried the stroke and fought back. Another blade sliced the half-light, then another. Aurelius reacted, leaping onto the terrace between columns, where he had a sure footing, and faced two screaming warriors whose glinting swords came at him from the sun-shafted gloom. He barely had time to wrap his cloak around his left forearm before they were upon him.

Verica shouted for help, as they fought desperately to counter the slashing blades of their assailants. With just the woollen material of his cloak and his sword to deflect the force of the blows, Aurelius could do little more than parry the slashes of his two assailants, unable to thrust back. He had left Excalibur behind and was fighting with a much shorter and broader gladius, better suited to defensive blocks. Verica managed to slash the legs of his assailant, causing him to fall to the ground. A flash of grey fur accompanied by a low growl signalled the arrival of Verica's two wolfhounds, followed by torchlight, shouts and running feet, causing the attackers to break off and attempt to flee. The dogs each jumped on a terrified warrior, causing them to stagger backwards in fright.

"Do not slay him and collar those dogs!" Verica shouted at his men, who had grabbed one stricken man from the wolfhounds. Others swarmed around the ruins with burning torches, probing into the darkness for the two who had run off. One lay dead, his throat ripped out by the determined and excited dogs.

"This one is a Saxon, my lord!" one of Verica's guards proclaimed, as Germanic oaths filled the air.

"Bring him to the fort for questioning. Come, Aurelius, let us leave this place."

Dishevelled but unhurt, the two nobles retired to Verica's hall, where he ordered goblets of sweet wine.

"My men will make him talk, and we have some who understand their language. This coastal area is dangerous, with Saxons and Jutes seemingly around every bend. It is possible they knew of our coming and were sent to kill us."

"How is that possible? It seems unlikely," Aurelius said, taking a large gulp of wine.

"It is credible that they have spies in Calleva, posing as tradesmen or cattle herders. We must be on our guard from now on," Verica muttered, scratching the heads of his hunting dogs. He noticed Aurelius looking at the pair of wolfhounds.

"These two great beauties were bred in Hibernia and are gifts from Triphun when they were mere pups. Now they stand with heads above my waist. They are keen hunters and can follow the scent of boar for miles. There are few wolves remaining in these parts, but plenty of boar and deer."

"And they are loyal to their master," Aurelius added.

The pair passed the rest of the evening exchanging hunting stories as they ate plates of meat and bread, content for the moment to put aside their worrying encounter. They would know more in the morning.

AFTER A NIGHT more comfortable than that spent by Verica's prisoner, Aurelius discovered that the man, in fact, was a Jute in the pay of Vortigern as a member of his foederati. The tribune's face was grim as Verica informed him that his suspicions had been confirmed. The man had confessed to being sent from a coastal fortress twenty miles to the west to find Aurelius and kill him, should the opportunity present itself.

Furthermore, Vortigern's spies in Calleva had already reported that an army was being assembled there.

As they prepared to ride out, Aurelius wrinkled his nose at a line of maggoty heads on poles, some with blond plaited hair waving in the morning breeze, surmising that the spy's head would soon join them. Now he knew that Vortigern had plans to kill him, he must be more alert. They were heading for Portus Adurni, the most westerly of nine coastal forts built by the Romans to garrison the troops who repelled seaborne invaders.

The horsemen picked their way through an undulating landscape of sand dunes sitting like round dumplings on the coastal plain, tasting the sea salt in the air. All was silent apart from the gentle moaning of the wind, the cry of gulls and the jangle of harness. They would from time to time pass by settlements, into which Verica would send a rider to ask about the movement of the Jutes. The small band of four riders had passed through two days before, but there had been little else since then. They mounted high headlands, towering over rocky cliffs and silently surveyed the desolate landscape and empty sea.

Verica rode beside Aurelius. "My friend, it is now clear that Vortigern has given territories to the Saxon and Jute chiefs who do his bidding here. And they no doubt kill or enslave those of our fellow Britons who resist attempts to dominate them."

He spurred his horse on a little way and indicated for his confidante to do the same. "This stone fortress we ride to is in the most westerly part of our tribal lands, and I must confess that I have neglected to visit it in recent times. I ignored reports of Saxons landing. Some of my party are from that area and are anxious for the well-being of their families and neighbours."

Aurelius furrowed his brow. "Are the Saxons and Jutes charged by Vortigern with defending the shores from all-comers, I wonder, or will they form a welcoming party for their own kind?"

All talk ceased as they rode in single file through a salty marsh; startled birds took to the air as the high reeds brushed against their feet. Verica caught up with Aurelius after they had forded a shallow stream, glancing at the setting sun as it dropped behind a dark forbidding forest.

"Let us make camp here for the night. Our journey takes us through the forest before us for half a day's ride before coming to the castle."

Aurelius nodded and Verica gave the signal for his men to dismount. The damp evening thickened as steam rose where both mounts and riders gratefully relieved themselves. The jangles and thuds of unsaddling, the groans as backs were stretched and provisions unloaded, and the murmur of human voices would soon overlay the squawk and flap of nature.

"Tell me, what do you know of the castle?" Aurelius asked as he slid awkwardly to the ground and began to work the stiffness from his knees.

Verica jumped down from his cherished white stallion and allowed it to nibble the grass. "It was built a hundred and fifty years ago by a Roman general called Carausius. It is a sturdy stone-walled castle some one hundred paces per wall. Many of our people were forced to quarry the flat local stone and build with it. They ferried lime from the Isle of Vectis for mortar. It would take a large army with siege machines to capture Portus Adurni."

"And what of this Carausius?" Aurelius asked, already knowing some of the legend. He was regarded as a deserter and traitor to the Romans.

"Even then there was a growing threat of raids by Germanic and Gaulish tribes. Carausius was charged by the emperor to build a line of defensive fortresses covering the south-east corner of our island. He controlled several legions and a fleet of ships. A vast fleet. But the guard dog thought himself a bear. With a defensive shield to protect the island from invasion, and knowing the Romans would be troubled to re-take our land, he declared himself Emperor of Britannia." Verica ended on a flourish.

"Ha ha!" laughed Aurelius. "And pray tell, what happened to this Emperor Carausius?"

Verica studied his friend solemnly. "What happens to all self-proclaimed emperors?"

"Slain by his deputy commander?" Aurelius offered.

"Indeed," was the reply, "by Allectus, who swiftly made peace with the Romans. To be fair, Carausius lasted ten years and completed his ring of coastal fortresses. He fought naval battles with the Romans in this Gaulish Sea, which must have been a wonder to behold. He was the first self-styled Emperor of Britannia, and minted his own coins, many of which are still in use in these parts. Here, I have one in my purse." He produced a small, round, part-silver denarius with the head of Carausius on one side and a lion on the other. He spun it to his friend.

Aurelius looked impressed. "This is a noble legacy of his reign, but how much blood soaked the earth or turned the sea red in its making? I fear many will also die as a consequence of my coming," he mused.

He turned the coin over and read, "'Restorer of Britannia'. An attempt, no doubt, to appeal to Briton tribes for support. A clever and organised military commander can achieve much in ten years."

When he took the reins of their horses and made to go to the picket line, Verica paused to remark, "Let us hope that our next emperor will have the fortitude, vision and military skills of Carausius."

But Aurelius refused to be drawn into speculation and simply remarked, "We should focus on the task in hand. We will know more of Vortigern's schemes after we reach this Portus Adurni."

THE FOLLOWING DAY, they entered the hush of the forest and moved softly along worn tracks in single rank. Verica stopped them short of all clearings. His scouts checked the way ahead and guided them away from any human settlements. After half a day's journey, they came to the southern edge of the forest and caught their first sighting of Portus Adurni, its white stone walls standing out on a spit of land jutting into a vast natural harbour. A native settlement stood close by a dozen roundhouses with smoke circling from openings at the top of their conical thatched roofs.

Verica whispered to his friend, "Is it our intention to capture this castle from the Jutes, my lord?"

"Aye, we must," replied Aurelius, narrowing his eyes to look beyond the buttressed walls to two long boats moored on a wooden pier. "Now we make a plan."

"We cannot storm the castle," Verica said. "It is too well fortified. There is a deep ditch all around and the gates are well defended from above. Let us withdraw and send our scouts to the village to ascertain the numbers of Jutes within. Some of my men are from this area and are known here."

The scouts smoothed their way, as Verica had hoped. Approximately one hundred Jute warriors, their families and some slaves, mainly children, captured from local villages, it soon transpired, occupied the castle. In addition, fifty or so Jutes had moved out to occupy surrounding villages.

"The village headman has offered to assist us," Verica explained. "I proposed we attempt to gain access through the side gate facing the village. A pair of our men can approach with an ox cart, posing as traders. There shall be a further four armed men in the cart, hidden under sacks. Once inside, they can overpower the guards and open the gates for our men to ride in."

"A simple plan," mused Aurelius, "but it assumes the gate will be lightly guarded."

"According to our contact, the Jutes are lazy and often drunk, playing dice and carousing with women. The element of surprise is with us, but we must act now, before sunset, as we cannot trust to fate that we will not be discovered."

AURELIUS AGREED TO the plan. It had been an easy journey and the men were keen, but he could not dissuade Verica from leading the assault. Without further delay, Verica selected his best five men. They stripped off their chain mail, wrapped their swords in a blanket, and set off on foot, approaching the village in a casual manner. Aurelius moved the remaining men to the shortest point between the edge of the forest and the side gate of the castle, a distance of a hundred and fifty paces. This would be a dash at full gallop of barely a minute, and should be enough time to gain access.

Verica acquired an ox cart with some sacks and straw, and four of the men concealed themselves. He gave some coins to the village headman, who promised to raise the men of the village in support, in readiness to join in the slaughter of the Jutes and free their captive friends.

The ox was driven along a dusty track no more than fifty paces distance to the gate, where several villagers were about their errands. Verica noted that there were two Jute soldiers in chain mail vests and round helmets, barking orders through thick blonde beards knotted at the corners. He approached slowly, leading the ox cart and holding a wooden staff.

"Halt!" commanded the guard in the local tongue. "What business do you have here?"

"We have brought bales of straw for the stables, sir," Verica said, with a low bow.

"Let me see." The tall Jute prodded a few bales with the tip of his spear, and seemed satisfied. "Pass!" he commanded.

Verica, with his companion, led the cart through the open gateway, passing under a high stone arch into an open space beyond. There were a cluster of huts and a stable for horses to his right, and what looked like Roman barrack blocks to his left, similar to the ones in Calleva. Straight ahead, dominating the central area, was a large wood and daub hall with a thatched roof. His eyes darted to the defensive walls and located a stone staircase. He did not wait long, for a cry went up and men pointed in the direction of the woods. Aurelius was on his way.

"To arms!" shouted Verica, as his men tumbled out of the cart, unsheathing their swords. Jutes were now running from the hall and barrack blocks towards the gate. "Hold them back! Keep the gates open!" he shouted as they engaged with the guards.

The thunder of approaching horses grew louder, inspiring the six men as they hacked down the gate guards and fought wildly to keep others at bay. Traders ran from the mayhem as the cavalry stormed over the wooden bridge and through the gatehouse, the setting sun to their backs, shields raised to deflect the few arrows that whistled from the battlements. They had surprised their enemy and now engaged in bloody combat, shouting oaths to encourage each other as they hacked at the Jutes from their horses, with some dismounting to fight on foot.

The unprepared Jutes were outnumbered and no match for the well-armed, battle-hungry Briton and Amorican fighters, with close to sixty slain before the survivors threw down their weapons. The villagers streamed in, looking to release prisoners and slaves. Aurelius was keen to question the Jute chief, a squat, round man named Gorm, and ordered him guarded in the hall, whilst he and Verica supervised the disarming and herding of all other prisoners into a cattle pen. They counted fifty men, thirty women and as many children.

"Bind the hands of the men and sit them down," he ordered, "and set a watch on the gates. Verica, send a dozen riders to the port and secure those two long ships; we may have a use for them."

That evening, they treated their men to a feast of food from the castle stores and gave two cattle to the village to slaughter for their own celebration. The victors were in high spirits, and Aurelius dined with Verica and their sub-commanders in the great hall. He had Gorm brought to the table and tied to a chair to watch them eat and drink his fare. The giant Jute understood the Briton language well enough.

"Tell us how you came to this place, oh mighty, fat Gorm!" Aurelius demanded.

When the raucous laughter subsided, he replied, "Your lord and master, Emperor Vortigern, did give us this castle and surrounding lands. That makes you rebels for this act of war!"

"We have our own ideas of how this coast shall be defended," Verica said.

Aurelius wanted more detail. "What is the agreement you have with Vortigern? Are you to protect these shores from other raiders from your own lands?"

Gorm, looking deflated, answered his captor. "We are charged with guarding the coast from pirates and other Germanic and Gaulish raiders. We have a charter to settle this area and defend it for our own tribe, from Juteland. For this we owe our allegiance to Vortigern and must pay homage to him in cattle or coin."

"And what other men of yours are outside of this castle? Perhaps you have patrols in the area or other settlements?" Aurelius carved a piece of meat and popped it into his mouth, looking at his salivating prisoner.

"My lord, I cannot divulge such information..." he stammered.

"Then we will beat it out of you," thundered Verica, "or slowly roast you on a spit!" The rowdy soldiers shouted oaths and banged their pewter mugs on the table as the blood drained from Gorm's moon-shaped face.

Before long, Aurelius had all the information he needed and called a meeting with Verica. Gorm, bruised after a beating, was given food and drink and sent to the pen with the other prisoners.

"My noble friend," Aurelius began, "we have acquired a castle, and must now hold it. However, I must return to Calleva and prepare our army, as I fear Vortigern, once he hears of this, will march against us."

"What shall we do with the prisoners?" asked Verica. "There are too many to guard and feed."

"Separate out their best warriors and execute them," Aurelius commanded. "I am not fond of torture for no reason, my friend, so kill them quickly and display their heads if you must. The remaining men, women and children can be given over to the villagers to work on their land or go to the quarry as slaves. We will leave most of our men here, under our deputy commanders, and sail those long ships to Noviomagus. You must brief your commander to send out mounted patrols in the morning to look for the few remaining Jutes in the surrounding villages. They should take some locals as guides. They must also recruit and train those locals willing to take up arms to bolster their numbers. We have plenty of Jutish swords, spears and shields in the armoury."

In the morning thirty men and their horses boarded the long boats and rowed out of the harbour. Catching an easterly wind, they charted a course along the rocky coastline, making for the next natural port along the jagged and treacherous south coast, Noviomagus. From there it was a full day's ride to Calleva where there was much to discuss.

5. The Battle of Guloph

THEY WATCHED IN respectful silence as the ball of orange sank behind a line of dark trees. The pink sky above, dotted with twinkling stars, seemed to celebrate the passing of a noble warrior and leader, as the glowing embers of the funeral pyre died down.

"Perhaps he is one of them," Cordelia sighed, following her son's gaze beyond the twisting smoke.

"He was the first to organise resistance, but not the last," Aurelius said, his arm around her shoulders, pulling her frail frame to him.

"Marcus has shown us the way," King Belinus growled, "and we must now look to our defences."

Aurelius stared at the mound of smouldering ashes. "You are wise, my lord, and know that Vortigern's army will soon be upon us. I fear my coming may bring death and destruction upon you all."

The portly Belinus pulled back an embroidered sleeve and took Aurelius's arm, leading him away from the group of mourners. "Do not berate yourself, Aurelius. Your coming is merely the catalyst for our resistance to Vortigern's plans. No good will come of inviting these hordes of warlike Saxons, Angles and Jutish people to fight under his banner and settle our lands. It is our collective will that you lead our army and oppose Vortigern and his feodorati. What are your thoughts on our defence?"

He fixed his keen brown eyes on Aurelius, perhaps echoing a similar encounter to one that had taken place some thirty years earlier, when Belinus's father, Valorian, had turned to a young Marcus for the defence of the town.

"My lord," Aurelius replied, "I fear we may not be able to defend the town against a large army who will surround it on all sides. They will break down one of our four gates and slaughter us within. You are the last fortified town in opposition to Vortigern facing eastwards, and in a perilous position. My advice is that you abandon Calleva and move the people west, where they will find a safe haven and lands to farm. With Marcus's dying breath, he advised me to take the army to the nearest hill to our west, at a place called Guloph, and await Vortigern there."

Belinus's brow was creased with sorrow and dismay. "You speak these words so lightly, my friend. To abandon our home, the town we grew up in, defended by our fathers against the mighty Saxon warlord, Cerdric, is no small matter..."

"My king, we have but little time," Aurelius interrupted, in his new authority, closing the sad lament. "I know this is the best way for you to protect your people from wanton slaughter and to increase our chances of victory on the field of battle. We must defeat their army and turn them back, or the west will be at their mercy, divided up as the spoils of war for the likes of Queen Rowena and her father, Hengist. My lord, you must find the strength of your forefathers to make this bold decision."

The two men stood staring into each other's eyes, the ashes of Marcus, mixed with oak and birch, catching in their hair. The other mourners turned to watch, realising this was more than just idle conversation.

"Then this is what we must do," Belinus intoned, turning away and leading the procession back to the temporary safety of the stone walls of Calleva.

"MY DECISION IS final!" Belinus thundered, as he glared at the sullen townsfolk outside the senate building. "Time is against us, and we must prepare to leave this place now. Pack what belongings you can carry, and follow the road north. Those with livestock and grain must provide half to our army. Join the Portway and head west, to Aqua Sulis, where we will assemble on the plain before its gates. Our scouts tell me that Vortigern's army has left Londinium and is moving west. They will be here in two days. My men are already spreading the word to outlying farms."

"But why should we flee from our emperor?" a voice shouted above the hubbub. Murmurs of discontent rippled through the restless crowd.

Belinus replied swiftly, "Because our emperor has employed Saxons to fight for him, the same Saxons you witnessed fighting our men in the arena. They are looking for land to settle, land promised to them by our Emperor Vortigern. Your land! This is no game, my friends. They will have our land, as we are unable to defend this kingdom of ours. Will you stay here and be slaves to the Saxons?"

The dissenters fell quiet and there was shaking of heads.

The portly king's voice rang out over the grumbles of his people, stirring them into action. "Be ready to leave at first light, and my guard will escort you to safety!"

Reluctantly, the crowd dispersed.

Aurelius met with his commanders at the parade ground in the enclosed barracks.

"We march at first light, following a westward path towards the hill at Guloph. King Belinus and his guards will escort the townsfolk to Aqua Sulis and join us thereafter. We can delay the advance of Vortigern by a day by giving the illusion that Calleva is defended. For this I require a mounted troop of one hundred to man the walls and show defiance. It is a dangerous mission and lives will be lost, but I feel we will need the time for our battle preparations and for more warriors to flock to our banners."

"I will do it," Uther said.

"I will need you and Brian at my side, Brother," Aurelius replied. "No, it must be my deputy, Tomos, with fifty of our Amorican cavalry, and Brian's sub-commander with fifty of the local mounted archers."

"I will name my young deputy, Kay, to lead the archers," Brian said.

"Good, then let it be done," Aurelius replied. "Once the town is empty of people, they will bar the gates and man the walls. On the second night, they may attempt to escape and save themselves. May Jupiter and the Christian God watch over them."

CORDELIA AND HER household departed with hugs and tears, joining the trail of ox-drawn carts heading north. The three brothers assembled their men on the parade ground and started their march out through the west gate, followed by their own wagon train carrying war machines, supplies and camp followers. The procession daubed a stroke of brilliance onto the muddy autumn morning, and farewells mingled with the clip of hooves, creaks of timber and shouted orders. Anxious elderly townsfolk quilted the day's ride to Guloph with their blessings, but their grandchildren whooped at the sheer spectacle of it all.

Aurelius wore a silver chain mail vest beneath a black bearskin cloak and, in defiance of Vortigern, retained his Roman cavalry brooches and helmet with the purple plume. Excalibur hung by his side, and slung from his saddle was a shining round shield, edged in silver, with a round steel boss, upon which was painted his new emblem – a bear grappling with a dragon.

Beside him were Brian and Uther, in full battle armour, and behind them rode Verica and Drustan.

They were followed by three banner bearers, two with embroidered cloth draped from a cross-pole, depicting the bear and dragon, with 'Ambrosius' stitched in Roman lettering on one, and 'The Divine One', emblazoned on the other. Trotting forward beneath the head of a roaring dragon, which had been cast in bronze and mounted atop a long pole, came the third bearer, little more than a tow-haired boy. They wore the tawny black-spotted skins of wild cats, and drew gasps of awe from those townsfolk who saw them ride out of the barracks. A new addition for the cavalrymen was lances with small triangular flags of differing colours denoting each unit. They would take a full day to reach the hill at Guloph.

Before sunset their scouts returned at a gallop, pulling up in a cloud of dust and reporting that the hill was through the next copse. They pushed ahead, emerging out of the woods to startle the locals in a small cluster of wattle and daub thatched roundhouses, whose flimsy picket fence was designed more to keep foxes away from their chickens than to keep out determined raiders.

Aurelius signalled for Verica and Drustan to come forward. "What is this place called?" he asked.

"Wallop, my lord," replied Drustan

"And what is the meaning of this 'Wallop'?"

"My lord," Drustan said, "in the local tongue it means 'the fast gallop of a horse'."

"I see," Aurelius replied. "Who are the people who inhabit these lands?"

"We are in the land of the Belgae, my lord, and these are my people."

"Then go and tell them what is about to befall them on this plain surrounding the hill. Offer them some coin for their livestock and grain, and try to recruit their young men as scouts. They must leave their houses, as soon a hostile army will be encamped here."

Verica offered, "Perhaps they can join our camp followers, my lord?"

"Yes, very well." Aurelius smiled at his warm-hearted friend.

"Very good, my lord, it shall be done," Drustan said, signalling to his followers and peeling away from the group.

"Ha! Then we shall wallop to the foot of this hill!" Aurelius quipped, spurring Perseus onwards. "Advance!"

The gently sloping grassy hill was a round dumpling dropped on the otherwise flat land. It had a sparse covering of heather and thorny bushes, and a small copse of birch on the western slope. They took their time riding up to the summit, following a goat herder's path, slowly picking their way between rocks and bushes. There was no evidence of structures, just a crude stone circle and patches of scorched earth, suggesting occasional use as a site for rituals. It commanded views for miles in all directions, save west, where a fringe of trees blocked the outlook.

"This was once a sacred place for the Druids," Drustan told Verica, breathing hard, having galloped to join the leaders.

"Then let us hope the ancient gods smile upon our cause," Verica remarked.

"Marcus was right," Aurelius said as he dismounted. "This is the place to receive Vortigern's army. Have the remaining heather cleared and a camp set up before those trees on the western slope. Clear the centre of the copse for a stable and use the timber to build corrals for the livestock. Tomorrow we look to the west for reinforcements, and to the east for the enemy."

Aurelius's six Roman engineers organised details of woodcutters and labourers who began work immediately on felling trees and removing the wood from the centre of the copse. The infantry was tasked with clearing the heather and then pitching the tents of a forward command post after dark. Canvas tents soon covered the cleared campsite, where fires roughened the air with their smoke and then sweetened it as the parcels in their peaty embers sizzled or baked.

Aurelius and his commanders patrolled the hilltop, teased by the wafting warmth of roasting boar. When they at last sank onto a log to eat, they discussed tactics as they slaked their thirst with mead and watered wine.

THE TOWN OF Calleva had stood for many hundreds of years, long before the coming of the Romans, who waged war on the Atrebates tribe, defeating them and taking over their capital, replacing the wooded fence surrounding the town with a high stone wall. The Romans had pacified them and re-named the town after them, calling it Calleva Atrebates. They had learned to live side by side with the Roman legions, allowing their sons to be recruited into their auxiliary forces.

Now it was deserted, with dust eddies swirling along its four main roads that led to a dry fountain in the central square. A few abandoned dogs sniffed about, running from the soldiers who had harnessed horses to the two oldest catapults to pull them to the north gate. Tomos and Kay were preparing their defences as best they could, and would use the Roman catapults to fire burning, pitch-soaked rocks over the walls.

"My lord," shouted a sentry at the north-west tower, "an army approaches!"

All one hundred men ran to the parapets and gazed out at the dust cloud gathering to the east. Soon the dreaded sound of Saxon war drums could be heard, growing louder by the minute. The late afternoon sun was to their backs as they watched the vanguard emerge from the forest. They had done all they could to make ready for a merciless onslaught, making full use of the day to prepare torches along the walls and ready their weapons. Their horses were saddled and tethered in groups close to the west and south gates, in readiness for their escape.

"When they come to talk with us, they will realise that Aurelius is not with us," Kay said to his co-commander.

"Aye, that is true. I will tell them our lords are busy and I am officer of the watch," Tomos replied.

Over the next hour, a mighty army filled the plains around the walled town, whose sides measured three hundred paces in length. The bulk of the army remained in front of the north gate. As the sun set, Vortigern and his commanders rode forward.

"I am your Emperor! You shall not close your gates to me!" he thundered.

In the gloomy light on the parapet over the gate, Tomos decided to take a chance. "My lord Vortigern, I am Ambrosius, Roman tribune and elected defender of the people! I will not open the gates to you and your army of Saxon dogs, who will rape our women, kill our men and seize our lands! I know what you have promised your queen and her kinsfolk. You must return to the east and leave us to run our affairs in peace!"

Kay had to stifle a laugh and whispered, "Well said, Tomos! Your mimicking of our leader is very real!"

Vortigern raged, "You impudent dog! I should have killed you when I had the chance, like I killed your father some thirty years past! I will give you until dawn to change your minds and receive what is left of my mercy! Go and talk to my cowering uncle and your gentle senators! They will not welcome a traitor's death!" He turned his horse and led his chiefs back to their lines, where soon tents were put up and campfires lit all around the doomed town.

"At least we have his confession to convey to Aurelius that he was the murderer of his father. Now at least one of us must make good his escape to carry that news," Tomos said. He gave orders for the torches to be lit, belying the emptiness of their counterfeit Calleva.

"We must count their numbers in the morning light and also convey that to our leader," Kay added, wrapping his woollen cloak about him as a chill autumn wind whispered its ill omen.

TWO DAYS HAD passed on Guloph Hill and the camp, housing four thousand fighting men and another four hundred followers, had been well established. A dozen neat rows of canvas tents, each housing ten soldiers, was surrounded by crude wooden huts to house the additional men, women and stores. Aurelius and his commanders looked with concern to the east, as thin lines of smoke rose to the grey sky on the horizon.

"It is surely our town burning," Aurelius said. "Let us hope some of our men have escaped to bring us news of its final moments."

"My lord," Verica said, "allow me to ride part-way with a mounted troop to meet our fleeing comrades and fend off any pursuers."

Aurelius saw the eagerness in his blue eyes. "Aye, you and Brian both. Take your Briton riders and use your judgement if engaging the enemy. Do not take on a force larger than yours. I yearn for news of the last stand of Tomos and Kay at Calleva, and pray for their safe return. Go."

Spirits were lifted in the camp at the prospect of some action. A troop of two hundred riders was selected, armed with lances, swords, bows and arrows, and they were saluted noisily by their comrades as they headed down the hill and into the woods. Brian proposed that he fan out into the countryside with his men, who were familiar with the territory, whilst Verica proceeded along the road to Calleva.

Verica sent out his fastest riders, and it was only two hours later that they returned, panting as they gave their news.

"My lord, there is fighting ahead!"

"How many of the enemy?" Verica asked.

"We could not see, my lord, but there are dismounted troops fighting in a clearing!"

"Forward!" Verica commanded, urging his men into a full charge. They emerged from the forest path into the murky daylight and saw thirty or more of Vortigern's black-clad cavalry, lunging with lances and slashing with their swords at the shields of their surrounded comrades, who numbered no more than a dozen.

Verica rode hard for the centre of the melee, whooping as he aimed his lance at a startled rider. In seconds, his soldiers clashed with Vortigern's East Britons, thrusting, stabbing and slashing. The sound of shields clashing, horses whinnying, cries and oaths filled the glen. With overwhelming numbers, Verica's troops soon saw off their enemy, chasing those who tried to flee and cutting them down.

When it was over, Verica dismounted and approached the ragged group of survivors. There were faces he recognised, but his commanders were not among them.

"Hail fellows! What news of Calleva? What is your name, soldier?" Verica asked, approaching the biggest man remaining, who clutched a bloody sword and a crushed shield.

"My lord, I am Brutus, formerly an innkeeper of Calleva. We held out for a full day and, as the town burned, made our escape into the night in small groups, fleeing through the enemy lines from the south and west gates, following paths through the woods known well to us, and trying to shake off our pursuers. We were forced to make our stand here, as our horses were overtaken by our enemy. As you see, just eight remain out of fifteen of us."

"You are brave, Brutus, as are all your men. You were prepared to fight to the end! Come with us to Aurelius and give him your report." Verica yelled after his eager men, "Break off your pursuit! We return to our camp!"

More soldiers limped into Guloph in small groups during the remainder of the day, each with stories to tell of skirmishes and rescues of their comrades, including some who had been captured and were set free. In all, over thirty men of the defenders of Calleva returned to be feted as heroes and, to Aurelius's delight, Tomos and Kay were amongst them.

Aurelius offered his own wineskin to his loyal aide to drink, before listening to his report.

Tomos managed a weary smile. "My lord, we did as you ordered. I even fooled Vortigern into believing you were there by imitating your voice, under cover of darkness!" The men roared with laughter, releasing some of the tension.

"Very clever, but I will not ask you to repeat your trick!" Aurelius laughed. "Pray, continue with your account."

"My lord, Vortigern gave us until dawn to surrender. After I refused to open the gates to him, they started their assault, firing burning bolts at our gates with their ballistae. We replied with our own catapults, and fired arrows down on them as they charged the gates with rams. Their first attempt was to test our strength. They withdrew and attacked again at all four gates, thinning our defenders to just between twenty to thirty per gate." He paused to spit.

"Before long they broke through the north gate, where their forces were strongest, and we managed to contain them by firing a barricade. This burned for two hours, keeping them at bay, and as the sun began to fade, we made good our plan to escape, firing all remaining buildings and the east gate to slow them down. As night fell they withdrew to a distance to watch our town burn."

His eyes clouded at the memory and he took a draught from the wineskin. "It was then that we opened the south and west gates and rode out, splitting into groups as we rode through their defensive lines, slashing at them with our swords. Some of those who rode south may still be alive and I pray to God they will join us."

Aurelius slapped him on the shoulder. "That is a brave and noble report, Tomos, and you have succeeded well in your task. But tell me, what size is Vortigern's army?"

All eyes were on the muddy soldier as he thought before replying. "My lord, we estimated three thousand foot soldiers and two thousand cavalry. They had six ballistae for firing bolts, and no other engines of war. Their force appears to be mainly Britons with about two thousand Saxons."

"That is a sizable force, indeed. We almost match it with our four thousand here, but I hope for more to arrive from the west and south-west. Where is Elafius? Triphun? Brennus? Uther, send riders out to see if there are any coming to join us." Uther bowed and departed.

Aurelius dismissed the men and returned to his command post.

"Tomos and Kay, you will eat with us this evening. Brian, send out more riders to the east to keep watch for any advances from our enemy. This may be our last night of peaceful sleep."

Yet, Aurelius would not get a peaceful night's sleep, once Tomos told him that Vortigern had boasted of murdering his father, Constantine. The image of his noble father, slumped sideways on his throne, would not leave him. There was nothing more to be said, and Aurelius retired early to bed to be with his thoughts.

The following morning, after breakfast, the army was assembled and their commanders briefed. The combined Roman, Amorican and Briton infantry, bearing rectangular Roman shields, iron-tipped lances and gladius swords, were deployed in ranks near the top of the hill, facing east.

Three thousand soldiers were arranged in three rows, with the most experienced and battle-hardened in the front rank. It was important to keep the shield wall tight and impenetrable, with the second rank able to lift their shields high to deflect arrows, javelins and other missiles, and ready to step into the front row should any man fall.

Aurelius was flanked by his cavalry. To his right, Brian led his five hundred mounted archers, swift and lightly armoured; their task was to move quickly and harass the enemy where needed. To his left, Uther commanded his heavy cavalry, whose task was to engage the enemy horsemen and to crash into their infantry ranks. Both riders and horses wore armour to protect them in this close-quarter fighting. Their coloured pennants fluttered in the morning breeze as their mounts pawed the ground in anticipation of work.

Aurelius had prepared surprises for an army advancing up the hill, but his strategy depended on drawing them to make an attack on his position. To this end, they had hidden part of their cavalry and their infantry reserves in the copse behind their camp. Also, they had their eight catapults concealed behind wicker screens, with distance markers measured to reach narrow channels containing pitch that would scour the hillside. All he needed was for Vortigern to oblige by advancing on his position up the east side of the gently sloping hill.

They waited patiently, flags and banners fluttering in the breeze, and soon heard the distant sound of war drums carried on the wind. Another handful of ragged survivors from the siege of Calleva arrived to cheer the troops, who quailed as a battle against an army bolstered by fearsome Saxons loomed.

Vortigern's scouts were seen entering the clearing from the woods, and minutes later their cavalry spilled out and rode through the huddle of abandoned brushwood shelters at the foot of the hill, smashing them down. Brandishing their spears and shields, they jeered at the silent army above them. Soon the infantry arrived and lined up facing them in two units – Britons and Saxons. Vortigern and his commanders sat behind on their horses, flanked by their cavalry, again divided into Britons and Saxons.

"Perhaps we are fighting two separate armies, my lord," Verica dryly remarked.

"Aye, and perhaps that could be to our benefit, if we strike hard at one side," Uther growled.

Aurelius considered this and asked, "Can we assume the Briton shield wall will be weaker? If so, then maybe Uther's cavalry could attack them from the left, causing their formation to break and allowing our infantry to get amongst them."

"Aye, my lord," Verica said, "and our strongest soldiers should move to the right to confront the Saxon shield wall?"

"Hmmm, you have a point, my friend. Our Roman legionaries and Amorican auxiliary have battle experience, which will count for much. Pass the word. Order our sub-commanders to move the Roman and Amorican soldiers to the right, opposing the Saxons. Brian's mounted archers shall harry the Saxons from the right, whilst Uther's cavalry charges into the Briton ranks to our left. This is our tactic, but first we must hold our ground and wait for them to advance on us. Vortigern will be mad and eager for our blood. Let him come."

A scout rode up to Aurelius from behind the hill. "My lord! Riders approach from the west!"

Aurelius dispatched Verica and Drustan to identify them as friend or foe. Just then, ahead of them, Vortigern and his deputies rode forward, indicating a desire to talk. The emperor and his mighty warhorse merged, under their polished mail and purple finery, into one formidable figure.

Aurelius turned to Constans. "I am of a mind to wait to hear news of these riders. When I am ready, I will meet Vortigern, with you, Brian and six of his archers, to hear his terms. Uther, you shall remain here to lead our army, in case of treachery."

Uther nodded his assent, and they remained unmoved for five minutes, keeping their emperor waiting. Verica and Drustan returned at a gallop, reining in before a shower of dust.

"My lord!" Verica shouted. "There are over five hundred riders and some retinue under the banners of Belinus, Elafius and Triphun! They have come to boost our numbers!"

"Excellent news, my friends!" Aurelius laughed. "Ride back and give them my greetings, and tell them to keep their men in reserve by the copse. Their commanders should ride forward and join Uther and wait for our return. Now I go to meet Vortigern!"

They rode gently down the slope, past sombre ranks of soldiers, and faced their emperor at ten paces.

"It is not good manners to keep your emperor waiting, Tribune Ambrosius," Vortigern barked as they approached, bearing his teeth to his retinue to elicit their smirks.

Aurelius took in the fierce group of six commanders whilst considering his reply. His eyes scanned from left to right, recognising King Jago and King Gorbonuc, and dwelling on the large, imposing figures of two Saxon chiefs he took to be Hengist and Horsa, their blond beards twisted into plaits. "Your subjects in the west are not happy with your alliance with those we consider our enemy," he said in a low, even voice.

"Then we are at odds, it seems," Vortigern casually replied, drawing sniggers from his men.

"Indeed, Vortigern. I see you have a new sword," he quipped, nodding to his side.

Vortigern's face flushed with anger. "You shall not mock me, Roman! I am emperor of all these lands and will crush those who oppose me! I need no fancy sword to cut off your head!"

"We will not yield to you, sly murderer of my father! Yes, I have heard of your guilty boast from our men who escaped Calleva. I intend to make you pay for it. If you wish to crush our small army, then try your best. But know this, we are ready to fight, to the last man, for this land and our freedom!"

"We agree on one thing," Vortigern said through gritted teeth, his black eyes glittering with malice. "Your army is small and made up of mere farmers. We will take little time in crushing you, and enjoy doing it!"

Aurelius turned away with the threats of Vortigern echoing after him.

"Your coming has exposed the traitors in my kingdom, and I will kill you all!" he thundered.

Constans rode beside Aurelius and whispered, "You have succeeded in raising his blood, my brother. Now he is angry!"

"And that is what we want," Aurelius replied, "for them to attack us on this hill."

On their return to their hilltop command post, Aurelius dismounted to greet the royal figures of King Elafius and King Belinus, and Triphun's nephews, Owain and Cadeyrn.

"Greetings, Aurelius!" Belinus puffed. "We have added a further five hundred horsemen to our cause, including the skilled cavalry under Cadeyrn, Prince of the Silures."

"This is excellent news and very timely. It matches our numbers to that of Vortigern. We hold the high ground and retain the element of surprise, unless his scouts have seen your approach. Let our noble princes and their cavalry remain in reserve, in readiness to join the fray on my command. What news of King Brennus?"

Belinus's face darkened, "Brennus will sit on the sidelines to see who prevails. He will not join us. Also, Mark, Duke of Cornubia, has stayed away."

"No matter," Aurelius lightly replied. "Now we wait for Vortigern's advance on our position. Make ready!"

Verica spoke up. "My lords, perhaps it is time to publicly elevate our leader to Ambrosius, The Divine One, sent by the gods to free us from tyranny."

"Very well," Belinus said. "Verica, proclaim it loud before the troops, and our new leader shall parade before them with his banners unfurled. Henceforth, he shall no longer be Aurelius, but shall be called 'Ambrosius'."

Ambrosius and Constans exchanged looks.

"Go, Brother, and fulfil your destiny," Constans said, with an affectionate smile.

Verica rode ahead of Ambrosius, standing up in his stirrups and rousing the men-at-arms to cheer their leader. Ambrosius rode behind, sitting tall on his snorting black stallion, the low autumn sun shining off his armour and helmet visor, lifted to reveal his sharp and intense brown-eyed stare. His standard bearers following behind, their banners rippling as they faced into a westerly wind that blew through the open mouth of the elevated bronze dragon head, making an eerie sound, as if a sleeping dragon was being roused from its long slumber.

The mood changed from one of quiet anxiety to determination as his army took up the chant, "Hail Ambrosius!" whilst beating their spears against their shields as he passed along the line. Most had not seen battle on this scale, and they swallowed their fears as they cheered their bold leader.

As Ambrosius and Verica resumed their positions, Ambrosius confided in his friend. "I willingly accept this role of divine leader and feel the power of it. I believe the gods have sent me to lead these people to victory over their cruel emperor. And I cannot deny the longing I have to avenge my father's murder by slaying Vortigern."

"Which of the gods do you worship?" asked Verica.

"Today, all of them. In deference to Marcus, I made sacrifice to Jupiter and Mithras before leaving Calleva, although I now feel the growing power of Christianity within my breast.

As if to confirm his words, Ambrosius called forth the priest from Calleva, Father Andreus, to give a blessing, in an open display of piety. The kings, princes and commanders dismounted and knelt to receive a blessing, after which Ambrosius embraced them all and dispatched his military commanders to their positions. The message was clear: God is on our side.

The Saxon war drums had struck up their ominous beat. Bronze horns rasped and purple banners fluttered as the front ranks of Vortigern's army began their slow, steady advance. To one side, from thick patches of marsh grass, a flock of orange-legged birds set up a piping alarm call as they rose to the air, the trailing black margin of their wings like an omen.

AMBROSIUS SAT IMPASSIVELY as his stallion snorted and pawed the ground. His commanders roused their soldiers to shout oaths and bang their axes, pitchforks and spears against their shields. Then something unexpected happened.

"My Lord! The Christians are marching on the enemy!" Tomos said, pointing away to their left.

Sure enough, the two bishops, Germanicus and Lupus, rounded a hillock. They led a group of a dozen tonsured monks, who carried banners depicting the face of Christ and their most

85

potent symbols – the chi-rho and the alpha and omega. Fifty or
so hymn-singing Christians followed them. They were walking
straight towards the Saxon flank of Vortigern's marching army.

"Those damned fools will be slaughtered. An ugly sight for
our men to witness!" fumed Belinus.

They watched on helplessly as the drama unfolded barely
four hundred paces from their position. Germanicus stopped,
raised his arms towards the advancing Saxons and declaimed
with passion, his words taken by the wind. The far-right section
of the Saxon flank stopped, and they faced up to the Christians,
as if facing a deadly foe, barely thirty paces from the preaching
holy man. Ambrosius could not hear what was being said, but
he could guess. He called the priest to his side and asked, "What
is happening, Father Andreus?"

"I know not, my lord," the distressed priest replied, "except
to say that rumours came to my ears that Bishop Germanicus
planned a bloodless march to preach God's word to our
enemies."

"The fool's going to get himself killed, but we cannot
intervene," Ambrosius replied solemnly. "Let God's will be
done."

The group of Saxons who had detached themselves from
their ranks now advanced menacingly on Germanicus and the
Christians, battle-axes in hand. Having covered half the
distance, they all appeared to stop, drop their weapons and go
down on their knees.

A cheer went up from Ambrosius's soldiers at the sight, and
word quickly spread to the rear ranks. Tomos shouted in joy and
made the Christian sign of the cross. "My lord! The Saxons have
fallen to their knees before the saintly Germanicus and thrown
down their axes! It is a miracle!"

King Elafius added, "Yes, it is another miracle from the holy man! He has cured my crippled son, who now walks as a result of his prayers!" The leaders all looked at Elafius in awe.

The advance continued. Other Saxons approached their prostrate comrades and heaved them forcibly to their lines. Germanicus continued to preach at them, his arms held outwards, as they withdrew under the orders of an animated mounted commander.

"We have been given a sign, my lord!" Tomos shouted in joy.

"Indeed we have," replied Ambrosius. He could see that the pitch markers had been reached by the enemy advance, and gave the signal for their catapults to be uncovered and their missiles lit.

"Fire!" he yelled, and eight burning balls were sent arcing through the air, over the heads of their own soldiers, landing amongst the startled front ranks of Vortigern's infantry and igniting the turf beneath their feet. "Cavalry, charge! Shield wall, prepare to advance!"

"God has blessed our cause!" Belinus cheered as he waved his sword above his head.

They watched from the hillside as the headlong rush of Uther's cavalry crashed into the ragged side of the Saxon formation, where those milling about close to the Christians were cut down ruthlessly. Germanicus, on seeing the yelling horsemen charging into battle, waved his followers to withdraw to the safety of the hillock.

In the centre ground, Vortigern's soldiers moved beyond the fires and their fallen comrades, and were driven up the hill by their commanders. Ambrosius lowered his raised arm, signalling the advance of his own soldiers and in less than a minute the two ranks of yelling soldiers clashed shields. The Roman legionaries and Amorican auxiliaries held firm and soon began to push back the Saxon line, making the most of their hilltop advantage.

The right flank of the Saxon wall was in disarray after the incident with Germanicus, followed by Uther's cavalry charge, and hand-to-hand fighting had broken out between Saxons and the horsemen. This allowed the legionaries to break through and succeed in stabbing with their short swords as the Saxons swung their battle-axes, roaring their defiance.

On the far right of Ambrosius's position, the two ranks of Briton warriors had locked their shields and pushed against each other, as javelins were thrown and arrows fired over the top at both sets of rear ranks, forcing them to lift their shields high.

"I see our Briton shield wall is better trained than our ragged foes," Constans shouted to Ambrosius above the noise of battle.

Brian's archers were busily harassing their opponents' flank, and engaging with their cavalry, who had been ordered onto the battlefield by Vortigern.

Ambrosius sent for the reserve forces, seeing an opportunity for a decisive victory, and soon Prince Owain and Prince Cadeyrn cantered their rested troops into the fray, spreading dismay amongst their seemingly overwhelmed opponents. He studied, in the distance, Vortigern and his personal escort, first watching on and then spurring their horses into a gallop.

"I think our emperor is stung by our attack!" shouted the diminutive Elafius, standing up in his stirrups.

"I think not, my friend," Ambrosius replied. "See, they are circling the fray and are making for our position. Make ready!"

Ambrosius, Belinus, Elafius, Constans, and their combined personal escorts, some thirty seasoned warriors, prepared to meet their enemy. Within a matter of minutes the two groups clashed. Battle cries and crashes of sword and shield echoed on the hill.

Excalibur was unsheathed and flourished aloft, shining in a shaft of afternoon sun. Ambrosius raised his shield and spurred his spirited mount towards the tyrant emperor. Vortigern's black-clad guards blocked his path pitching Ambrosius into a duel against a burly bodyguard. When a cry went up beside him, he turned to see the stricken figure of the portly Belinus tumble from his saddle.

"The king is down!" shouted one of his retainers.

Vortigern's bodyguard saw his opportunity and lunged at Ambrosius, who swiveled towards him at the last moment, deflecting his blow with his shield. Excalibur was ready to bite, and he drove the blade into the exposed neck of his surprised opponent, killing him in an instant.

The skirmish was in deadlock. Vortigern, seeing no way of getting to Ambrosius, ordered a retreat, and his force fled back to their position. Ambrosius did not give chase, instead dismounting to attend to the King of the Atrebates, now lying flat on his back. Elafius and Constans were loosening his armour, exposing a gaping and bloody sword wound.

"He is dying, my lord!" Constans wailed, cupping the aged king's head in his hands.

Ambrosius saw his precious mentor's eyelids flutter one last time. Marcus first, and now, Belinus. He felt a sudden pang of sorrow and the realisation he was now alone with the burden of leadership.

Constans stood and saw his brother's look of dejection as the battle raged close by.

"He is dead, my brother, but you must lead this army. Come, let us ride into the fray and urge our soldiers on!"

The brothers clasped arms and swiftly mounted, leaving Elafius and Belinus's retainers behind, and swept down the hill with their escort. The shield walls had broken down and hand-to-hand combat was all about them, as screaming and bloodied men threw themselves at each other. Ambrosius drove into the melee, slashing to his sides with Excalibur, his bannermen close by, signaling his presence on the field of battle. Soon, Brian and Uther had fought their way to his side, and their troops were heartened at the sight of the four brothers fighting valiantly.

"Look, my lord!" Tomos shouted, pointing over the heads of the combatants to Vortigern and his men, who were quietly retreating to the forest. "We have won the day!"

Vortigern's ragged and battered army disengaged and followed their leaders towards the woods, chased by horsemen who mercilessly hacked at them. At the sight of Saxons fleeing the field, Ambrosius's triumphant warriors set about dispatching the dying and collecting trophies.

Constans could see his brother straining to see where Vortigern had gone, standing in his stirrups and pulling anxiously at the reins of his mount.

"Now is not the time for vengeance, my brother. Let us make good our victory and then look to pursue Vortigern."

Ambrosius scowled at him, but nodded his assent.

Some of the Briton warriors who had been fighting for their emperor gave up and threw down their weapons. Commanders Drustan and Verica looked to Ambrosius, who nodded his assent that they should show them mercy.

"Recall your riders," Ambrosius shouted to Brian, Uther and Caydern, "the battle is won."

Skirmishes still raged around the clearing before the screen of trees, but within two hours of the first clash of shields, it was all over. Bodies lay strewn across the mud-churned pasture between hill and trees.

"You have won a famous victory, Ambrosius!" Verica exclaimed, back at their hilltop camp. "It is Vortigern's first defeat in battle in more than twenty years of his rule! All hail Ambrosius!"

The shout was taken up, and Ambrosius paraded with his banner bearers before his cheering army.

"Aye, and the biggest battle this island has seen since the days of the Roman legions," Drustan remarked as they followed in procession.

King Belinus was dead, and would be mourned, and two nobles wounded. In addition, over a thousand soldiers were dead and several hundred wounded. But they had killed over half of Vortigern's army, including close to a thousand Saxons, whose blonde heads were much-prized trophies.

Tomos and Uther were absent. They had ridden to the place where Germanicus had preached to the Saxons, and then escorted the bishops and their dishevelled followers to their camp.

Later, Uther joined Ambrosius and had a quiet word.

"My noble brother, the miracle of Germanicus can be explained.

Ambrosius raised a brow in query and waited.

"As you know, I learned the healing properties of common plants at the knee of our grandmother, Morcant; knowledge I intend to pass to my daughter, Morgana."

"Aye; I remember the old woman taking us to pick plants from the forest. What of it?" Ambrosius asked, chewing on a chop.

Uther continued. "I noticed patches of the bright moss that can be dried to cover wounds. Closer to the scene, I saw black rushes. And the truth of the miracle was then clear to me."

His listener shrugged his shoulders, still waiting.

"There is a peat bog down there, Brother, where the Saxons sank in, up to their knees. From our position, it looked as if they were kneeling before the holy cross of the Christians. Look there, at the trails in the mud where their comrades pulled them out."

Uther pointed, and Ambrosius, squinting in the half-light after sunset, let out a laugh, slapping him on the back.

"There is often an explanation for these so-called miracles, and you have found it, my brother! But let us keep this between ourselves and Tomos, as our soldiers now believe they fight for a just and divine cause. We shall keep Germanicus and his followers with us, for we need to draw more locals to our banner, and to the banner of Christ's followers. Our fight is not over. We have wounded Vortigern this day, but have not defeated him."

6. The Saxon Menace

VORTIGERN GAZED THROUGH the murky stained glass window into a hazy green and crooked courtyard. Saxons were dismounting from their horses. The great hall of what was once the Roman governor's palace in Camulodunum was a huge, empty and sombre space, save for servants scurrying with goblets and platters to appease their unhappy emperor.

"Find my counsellors! Bring them to me! I do not wish to face these brutish Saxons and their constant demands alone!"

Barely a week had passed since the unexpected reversal of fortunes at the Battle of Guloph. In that time, Vortigern had been obliged to release his chiefs and kings to return to their lands in order to quell any disturbances prompted by the rebel victory. Queen Rowena had soothed him, scarcely mentioning that a fleet of a dozen ships bearing more Saxon warriors and their families had arrived at the Isle of Thanet colony.

"My lord Hengist, and brother Horsa, welcome!" Vortigern's voice echoed across the hall as the delegation of eight strode across the floor to his raised throne.

"Greetings, my king, Vortigern," Hengist replied in a harsh Germanic accent. "May I present my cousins, Ella and Grimwold, who have come to aid us in our fight against the northern men."

The bearded warriors bowed, and Vortigern managed a half-smile as he nodded.

"Please, take a seat and we shall drink some fine mead made by our monks," he said, guiding his visitors to an oak banquet table. He knew the mood of the Saxons would mellow with a mug of mead in their hands. Vortigern glanced around for support from his nobles, but none were present.

During their small talk, Vortigern elicited the fact that over three thousand Saxons were now settled on Thanet. In the silence that greeted this news, Hengist cleared his throat, preparing to unveil the purpose of his visit.

"My lord Vortigern, our numbers have grown beyond the ability of that small island to contain us. We wish to move south, beyond the marshes, to settle in the kingdom known as Ceint. Will you grant us your favour and allow us to settle this area? From there we can better mount opposition to your rebels."

Vortigern fixed his black eyes on the huge, scarred face of the blond-haired warrior chief and stared into his blue eyes, seeing nothing but confidence and mild contempt. He knew they would do it anyway, and cursed himself for his weak position.

"My lord Hengist, the Kingdom of Ceint is already partially occupied by your neighbours from Juteland. I hear that the King of Ceint, Corangon, has fled westwards. I see no reason why I cannot grant you this kingdom, and charge you with protecting our south-east shore from unwarranted incursions. However, you must make peace with the Jutes, many of whom are part of my foederati and man our coastal defences."

Hengist laughed and clashed pewter mugs with his brother and cousins. "Well said, my emperor!" he jeered. "We will march to Cantiacorum and bring the Jutes to heel. I know their leader. They are no match for our might, and I will make my base there, where the Romans once kept their legions!"

Vortigern gritted his teeth, sensing the growing power of his father-in-law. Half of his Briton army had been slain by Ambrosius, some had been captured and his nobles were wavering. The Saxons had suffered a setback, but were now supplementing their numbers with new arrivals. In contrast, his position was weakening by the day.

Rowena entered and greeted her father, uncle and second cousins, finally coming to her sulking husband. "My king, what ails thee?" she trilled merrily. "Is the company of my family not to your liking?" The Saxons roared with laughter as Vortigern's face turned red.

"My lady," he said, through gritted teeth, "I am enjoying their company very much, and now yours as you have lighted up the hall. Come and sit next to me." The tall blonde beauty swayed her hips seductively as she went to sit on the arm of his chair. She then ran her fingers through Vortigern's black hair as the Saxons sniggered.

"My lord, I have taken the liberty of arranging a feast in your honour," she said. "To this end, I sent out an invitation to your chiefs, carried by your messengers, to attend on the morrow. I hope this pleases my lord." She smiled and stared into his eyes, pulling him towards her and gently kissing his lips.

"Of course, my dear. A celebration is what we need. More mead!" Vortigern hid his concern and growing paranoia, comforted by the thought that with his nobles around him he would feel more secure. News of the movement of the rebel army and the Atrebates tribe to the west after his rout at Guloph had not yet reached him.

AMBROSIUS AND HIS commanders had huddled around the embers of King Belinus's funeral pyre, which glowed red against the evening sky, on top of the hill at Gulloph. They were still in their encampment the day after the battle, weary after burying the dead in huge pits dug by their prisoners. Some four hundred of Vortigern's warriors, mainly from the Iceni and Corieltanui people, had sworn an oath of allegiance to Ambrosius, sensing a change in Briton politics. They had little liking for the Saxons and feared losing their homesteads to them. One hundred Saxon warriors were now in chains, and Ambrosius resisted his urges to have them killed.

Germanicus took Ambrosius to one side. "My son, God has smiled on your cause, and will continue to do so as long as you and your men desist from acts of barbaric cruelty and embrace the cross of Our Lord Jesus Christ."

"We have spared many, killing only the wounded as is the way in warfare," Ambrosius replied evenly.

"It grieves me to see the heads of dead warriors displayed on poles by some of your followers. Such practices belong to the pagans and are at odds with the teachings of our holy church," Germanicus admonished.

Ambrosius pondered for a moment. "I am also of a mind to ban this act of head collecting, but I would not offend men who see it as their victor's right and an act of vengeance against invaders who have caused much suffering. I pray you, do not stir up discontent with my men, Father. Later, I will speak privately on this with Verica, a chief with much influence."

The bishop's nod of acceptance was acknowledged before Ambrosius briskly turned to weightier matters, summoning his commanders to him. There were things to be said.

"Dear friends we have won an important battle against Vortigern and his followers, showing our strength and resolve to the Saxon invaders." Cries of 'aye' rang out from the group. "We will leave this place tomorrow, and many of you will return to your lands to be welcomed as heroes. But this is only the beginning of our campaign. There will be more fighting before Vortigern is finally defeated and removed from power, and the Saxons are pushed back into the seas!"

He eyed the cheering group of loyal followers before continuing. "King Belinus's son, Eliduris, now the chief of the Atrebates, will lead his people to Aqua Sulis, under my banner, to make new homes in the west." He put his arm around the slender shoulders of a thin and pale youth, swamped in his father's large red cloak. "We cannot abandon the defence of these lands, and must deploy our soldiers in coastal forts and to the borders of Ceint in the east. In this regard, Verica, Drustan, Uther and Brian have agreed to be area commanders." Cheers went up and arms were gripped in approval of the valiant leaders.

Ambrosius held up his hands for quiet. "I have also agreed to ride north to the court of King Brennus in the company of King Elafius, so we may know his intentions..." There was some commotion behind the line of commanders, distracting Ambrosius. He was surprised to see the group part to make way for the bishops, Germanicus and Lupus, leading a procession towards him. Behind them came Father Andreus, carrying something in his arms, out of view of the curious Ambrosius.

Germanicus turned and hushed his swelling congregation before addressing Ambrosius.

"Today, I have been charged by this group of nobles, here assembled, to anoint our noble commander and Roman tribune, Ambrosius Aurelius, as King of the Britons!"

A huge roar of approval went up from the crowd, as the bishops parted to allow Andreus to step forward, carrying a red cushion on which sat a plain gold crown.

"Do you, Ambrosius Aurelius, accept this charge to lead the people of Briton and be their king?"

For a fleeting moment, Ambrosius's composure wavered. "I am taken by surprise at this unexpected honour. Yes, I will accept your charge to be your leader and high king of the Britons, but am mindful of the fact that Vortigern is still at large and bears the same title."

"Not for long!" shouted Uther. Cheers rang out and swords were waved in the air as Ambrosius went down on one knee before Germanicus who placed the crown on his head.

"Before God and with this holy water, I anoint you King Ambrosius of the Britons, the Divine One whom God favours! May you live long and defend these lands from those who wish harm on our peoples. All hail King Ambrosius!"

The happy nobles retired to the ancient stone circle to enjoy a few hours' respite after the battle and before their trek westward the next day. They feasted on roast pig and small birds, drinking rowdy toasts from mugs of mead to their brave warriors and new king.

VORTIGERN'S FEAST TOOK place in a tense atmosphere, as the twenty or so sulking Briton nobles were forced to put aside their worries and eat with their joyous and rowdy Saxon allies. They had suffered a serious reversal at Guloph, some losing many men, although the Saxons seemed not to care. Queen Rowena had made a point of encouraging unity by seating each Briton noble between Saxon warriors. Hengist and Horsa sat next to each other to the right of Vortigern, on the top table, and Rowena sat to his left. Close by, the white-haired Bishop Morgan sat, looking uncomfortable, surrounded by the coarse Saxon pagans.

Roasted meats, served on platters beside flat bread and a mash of leeks and turnips flavoured with herbs, were washed down with pitchers of mead. At the head table, spiced wine was served, and soon merriment replaced suspicion as tales of valour in combat and feats of knife-throwing were traded between the two warrior nations.

Vortigern became drunk and moody, throwing bones and scraps at his eager hounds. Hengist and Rowena exchanged knowing looks as Vortigern was distracted, and the big Saxon pushed back his chair and stood. All the Saxons looked up at their leader as their merry neighbours prattled on, and Hengist drew his knife from his scabbard and held it above his head. This was the signal for his fellow countrymen to draw their own knives and plunge them into the startled Briton nobles.

Cries and some brief resistance broke out around the table. Stunned, Vortigern watched helplessly as all his men, taken completely by surprise, were butchered in front of him. Bishop Morgan was not spared, and he barely had time to offer up a prayer before his throat was cut from behind. Hengist and Horsa stood on either side of the struggling emperor, holding him down and forcing him to witness the final dying grimaces and groans of his assembled nobles, including King Jago and King Gorbonuc. A brief, deathly silence soon gave way to the defiant and victorious roars of the brutal flaxen-haired barbarians, who licked the blood from their knives and washed it down with ale.

Hengist stood in front of the terrified Vortigern and said, "My lord, your nobles and holy man are dead, and now your kingdom is mine. We will keep you here to put your seal to papers, but you will now answer to me!" The belittled emperor was led away by armed warriors to his chamber, as his entourage of retainers and palace guards were disarmed and locked up in the dungeons. Without ceremony, the dead nobles were dragged outside and piled onto a cart by Saxon warriors who then took up the posts of the deposed guards.

7. Cautious Alliances

AMBROSIUS AND ELAFIUS followed the Portway east until they found the longhouse of King Brennus, in the fortified settlement of Readingum, on a bend in the River Tamesis that flowed to Londinium. Their welcome was subdued as the gloomy king waved them to sit at his long table. Ambrosius waited to hear what their host had to say.

After ordering refreshments, Brennus said, "Welcome dear friend Elafius, and Tribune Ambrosius, who now wears the gold crown of a king around your helmet. We have seen many defeated warriors pass by our homes. Tell me of your victory over Emperor Vortigern. Do you come to chide me? Pray tell."

Elafius glanced at Ambrosius and elected to speak. "Hail, cousin, and our thanks for your welcome. You have heard we won a victory at the hill at Guloph, brushing aside the combined army of Vortigern and the Saxon hordes which trouble our land. But we missed your banner flying beside us."

Brennus smiled and nodded, acknowledging the diplomatic opening offered for his mitigation.

"My noble guests, I can offer no excuse except to say that when Vortigern's army passed by my gates on its way to meet you, I could not say I would not attend, out of fear of retribution. Instead, I said I would need time to gather my men and follow some days later. I did gather my meagre army, but did not join Vortigern in the sacking of my neighbouring town, Calleva, fearing that good King Belinus would be put to the sword. This was not a thing I wanted to be part of. Instead, I rode west along the Portway and camped in the woods, sending out scouts to inform me of events."

He paused to pour wine for his guests, waving his attendants away. "We moved close to your battlefield in the

Wallops, but I elected to remain on the sides, to await the outcome. I beseech you not to be angry with me, for my small group of barely three hundred men would not have swung the fight one way or the other. I had earlier sent a token of my support to you by sending three hundred of my guard. I pray you will not blame me, and understand the perilous position I was in. But I can now say I am happy for your victory and salute you!"

Ambrosius sat grim-faced and refused to lift his goblet. At last he spoke. "King Brennus, as you have seen, the nobles in the west of your island have made me their king. I have been charged with defending these lands from all invaders and those who befriend them. We would know your intentions. Will you join our alliance to overthrow Vortigern and drive these Saxons back to the sea whence they came?"

The two men eyed each other before Brennus replied. "I will not lie to you, 'King' Ambrosius. Today I will say to you that you are my king, but should Vortigern arrive with an army, then I will say the same to him. Though, I have refused to attend a banquet organised by Queen Rowena to bring together Saxon and Briton nobles. This may put me at odds with him..."

"But what is your preference, my friend?" Elafius pressed. "We would know if your position on this river is to be our outpost against a counter strike by our enemy. For us, there is no going back. We are committed to this rebellion, and will fight to overthrow Vortigern and make Ambrosius king of this island."

Ambrosius interrupted tersely. "You cannot say you are with us today and will be with Vortigern tomorrow. That is not acceptable..." Brennus flung back his chair and Ambrosius mirrored him. They faced each other, hands on their sword hilts.

"I am a king and you are in my court," Brennus hissed between gritted teeth. Elafius wedged his tiny frame between the two tall warriors. "My friends, let us not fight. Please sit and allay your anger."

Begrudgingly, they sat and Elafius continued his role as peacemaker. "Cousin Brennus, you must see our position as victors in a battle that has damaged more than Vortigern's pride. We killed half his army, and many captured Britons from your neighbouring lands have pledged their swords to us." Brennus was now agog. "Yes, my friend," Elafius continued, "nearly five hundred Corieltanui and Iceni warriors now follow our banners, and they are brothers to your Catwellauni people."

"This is news," Brennus said, sitting back in his chair and adopting a more relaxed posture. He stroked his pointed beard and said, "I will agree to join you, provided you double the size of my garrison and help to build my fortifications."

"Agreed," Ambrosius said, and they managed an awkward handshake.

"You will be my guests this night and we will celebrate your victory. And now, I swear my fealty to you, King Ambrosius," he said, bowing slightly with a tilt of the head.

The following morning, a merchant boat nosed its prow up river, through the mists of low-lying Londinium, and furled its sail by Brennus's quay at Readingum. It brought wine, colourful Gaulish pottery and lurid reports of the murders of Jago and Gorbonuc and many nobles from eastern and northern tribes. The merchants were unable to say if Vortigern was alive or dead, only that the Saxons controlled his court and were unchallenged rulers of southeast Briton. The townsfolk declared the tale to be beyond belief, but tethered their livestock and whetted their sickles.

As Ambrosius and Elafius prepared to leave, Brennus spoke to them. "Your visit is timely, and your cause indeed just and noble. There will be no more wavering from me on the matter. I will today sign an edict to be read to my people, telling them of the cruel slaughter of our neighbouring nobles and the imminent threat to us from the Saxon hordes, now free of their charge as the Emperor's foederati."

Ambrosius clasped his forearm in a firm salute and said, "King Brennus, with your help we will win this war, and can recruit more support for our cause as a result of this treachery by Hengist and Queen Rowena. Their goal of seizing this island, and subjugating the Briton tribes, is now clear and must be resisted. We will send warriors and Roman engineers to you to build your defences. God's blessings on you."

THEY PAUSED BY the turn-off to Calleva and stared wistfully down the road that led to the abandoned town.

"I imagine a hollow town with open gates, inhabited by ghosts and packs of scavenging dogs, and crows circling," Ambrosius said mournfully.

"It is a warning. An ill omen of things to come," Elafius replied. There was little more to say, and they spurred their horses westward on the dusty Portway.

They camped that night at the retired Roman legionaries' settlement, some twenty miles short of Aqua Sulis, and were pleasantly surprised at the well-kept houses and fields. They were afforded an eager welcome by the sons and grandsons of former soldiers and exchanged tales around their campfire with them well into the night. Ambrosius recounted the battle at Guloph Hill and told them of his intention to establish a strong kingdom in opposition to Vortigern and the Saxons. He was preaching to a converted audience, who all stood and applauded their new king's victory.

"You are a strong lad," Ambrosius remarked, eying a tall, muscular youth. "What is your name?"

The young man blushed and bowed slightly before replying. "I am Gawain, my lord. My grandfather was an optio in the Second Augustus Legion. I have lived here all my life and work the fields."

"I am of a mind to take you with me, young Gawain. Would you like to be one of my squires?"

The shy youngster stared downwards and shuffled awkwardly. "I might, my lord, but you must ask my mother, for I am the man of the house since my father's death this year."

"Then I will speak with your mother," Ambrosius replied.

"My lord, may I ask, what is a squire?" the youth stammered.

Elafius exchanged looks with Ambrosius and answered on behalf of his king. "A squire, my boy, is a youth who serves a lord or king. He may also serve a valued mounted warrior, proven in tournament or battle, who swears allegiance to a king. I am sure our new high king, Ambrosius, will require the services of many men with strong arms and brave hearts. Each mighty warrior requires a squire to tend to his needs, keeping his horse and weapons in good order."

Gawain was clearly impressed, and stood beaming by the firelight, as the visitors laughed and carved chunks of spit-roasted deer with their knives.

The following morning, they departed to cheers, with six young men added to their group. By afternoon, they had reached the plain before the walled town of Aqua Sulis, and heard a commotion before setting eyes on a great number of people with their livestock camped about them. They were welcomed by Eliduris, the new king of the Atrebates people, now comfortably attired in the manner of his noble father, but bearing a worried look on his young face.

"Come and ride with me, Eliduris," Ambrosius said, after they had broken bread together under the canopy of a yew tree. "We shall discuss our future whilst taking the healing waters. You say my mother and sister are well, but I would like to bathe before I visit their tent."

They entered the gates of the town and were cheered to the stone senate building, where Kinarius, the chief and their host, welcomed them to Caer Badon, the name by which the town and its environs were known locally. He was flanked by Verica, Uther, Brian and Constans. Ambrosius was pleased to see his brother Constans, nursing an arm in a sling, much improved from the treatment by Bishop Germanicus.

"Well met brother! I see your battle wound is healing. Where is our holy bishop?" Ambrosius enquired.

"He must soon return to Gaul, leaving Bishop Lupus with us. But first he has gone to the south and west to stir up the Christian churches, my kingly brother," Constans replied with a broad smile.

Brian added, "But not before preaching that our Atrebates will find their homeland, as did the tribes of Israel after fleeing Egypt and arriving at Jerusalem!"

"A worthy sermon, indeed!" Ambrosius laughed.

Presently, the group of leaders retired to the baths, where they disrobed and eased into the opaque emerald green water.

"You have maintained this bathhouse well, Kinarius, to Roman standards," Ambrosius quipped.

"My thanks, Lord. It is a matter of pride for the Dumnonii, who quarried the stone and built under Roman instruction, and now have inherited the town and surrounding settlements from our illustrious masters."

"And now you are the masters," Verica said, "and must show wise and strong leadership, taking what was best from Rome and weaving it with your tribal ways."

"Indeed," Kinarius said, cupping water in his hands and splashing it over his head, "we must all look to steer a path through these uncertain times."

All eyes turned to Ambrosius who dipped his head under the warm water and then surfaced, rubbing the stinging minerals from his eyes. He was not yet of a mind to talk politics. "Tell me of the water goddess whose shrine this is."

Kinarius gestured to his servants to bring platters of dried fruit and cups of wine for his guests. They walked down the steps into the water and waded to the group of a dozen men wallowing, naked, beside a marble shelf.

"This is a joint temple to the Roman goddess Minerva, whose statue you see before us, and our own tribal goddess of the rivers, Sulis, depicted in the frieze between these columns. Hence the naming of the town, 'the Waters of Sulis'."

"Indeed," Ambrosius said, "the Romans were always eager to please those people who submitted to their rule."

"As was the way with Calleva Atrebatum," the young King Eliduris said, mournfully.

"It shall rise again, my young friend," Verica replied, "once we have swept the Saxons from this land!"

In due course, their talk turned to their situation. Ambrosius looked at the expectant faces of his commanders and the three tribal leaders and spoke. "My dear friends, we have stirred the hornet's nest and must face what comes at us. We must resist the urge to run and hide. That will only result in us losing our lands and being hunted down like slaves who have fled their master."

He paused to allow some murmurs of agreement. "We must prepare the defences of our towns but also keep an army in the field, ready to engage the enemy. This war has just begun, and we must stay strong and united in our resolve, as leaders to our people. I wish to establish my base in these lands. I hear the Roman town of Corinium to the north is sparsely populated and in decline. Is that so, Kinarius?"

All eyes shifted to the local chief. "Aye my lord, it is so. The locals there are cousins to our tribe, but few are warriors and there is little will to take up arms. They flee to the woods, like squirrels, at the first whiff of riders, and their town has been heavily looted and pillaged for stone. They provide a barrier between us and Vortigern's home town, Caer Gloui, that controls the lands by a mighty river and passage by way of a toll bridge to the land of the Silures and the mountain kingdoms of Dyfed beyond."

"And what have you heard of Vortigern since the Saxons slaughtered his nobles?"

"My lord, only that he was spared and his queen, Rowena, now rules in the east. He is their captive, and we know not what his fate will be," replied Kinarius. "My lord, shall we talk in the anteroom where servant girls await to rub soothing oils into our bodies?"

"I shall soon know what it is like to be a Roman senator!" Uther growled.

Kinarius guided them out of the waters; a young toga-clad woman holding a linen towel met each of them. They were led into an adjoining room, to marble slabs covered with finely woven sheets. Here, they lay face down and their massages elicited groans of delight.

After some time, Ambrosius revealed his plans. "It is my intention to go with the Atrebates people to Corinium and settle there. However, noble Kinarius, I would welcome your thoughts on how well we would be received by the locals?"

Kinarius turned his head towards him and replied, "My lord, perhaps I should ride with you to talk with my tribal cousins. I am not even sure who their leader is, but I will surely be known to them. To settle a tribe of some one thousand, with livestock, is no small matter, and some negotiation will be needed to avoid conflict."

"That is an excellent suggestion. What say you, King Eliduris?"

"My lord and king, I am at your service. I must find a home for my people soon as they grow restless. Let it be so."

"Fine, we are agreed, let us not delay and start out tomorrow!"

The men sat up and allowed themselves to be dressed.

Uther took Ambrosius to one side as they walked between stone columns to leave the bathhouse. Brother, allow me to ride east with my cavalry to patrol our borders and make report of the ruin of Calleva."

Ambrosius stopped and faced him. "That can wait until we settle at Corinium. We may meet Vortigern's soldiers so close to his homeland."

Uther planted his feet apart, put his hands on his hips and raised his voice. "I disagree, my brother. We have over one thousand mounted troops. Half could accompany you north and half ride east with me..."

Verica, hearing Uther's demand, interrupted the glowering Pendragons. "My lords, if I may..."

"You may not!" thundered Ambrosius. "We shall all move on to Corinium!"

Uther would not back down and his face turned purple with rage. "You rule by consent, my adoptive brother! Do not push me too far..."

"Or what?" Ambrosius growled. Both men had their hands on their sword hilts.

They stared each other down for what seemed an age until Brian came between them.

"My brothers, let us not fight. We all want the same thing, so let us discuss it like men. Our dear father Marcus raised us as brothers, and so we shall remain!"

"There is nothing to discuss!" Ambrosius hissed.

"You have started to believe you are the Divine One," Uther said in a low, dangerous voice, "but I know you are just a man, like any other." He brushed past Ambrosius and stormed out of the bathhouse into the sunlight.

Ambrosius turned as if to follow, but was restrained by Brian and Verica.

"Let him go," Brian advised. "He is headstrong and angry at your rebuttal. It will not last."

"But he has defied me!" Ambrosius spluttered.

"He is your brother," said Verica in a soothing tone. "His loyalty to you is not in doubt."

"He called me 'adoptive brother', as if our ties were not so strong," Ambrosius said, walking away from them and out into the street of milling traders and herders, not sure which way to turn.

Kinarius appeared at his side. "This way, my lord, let us retire to my hall."

Uther sat with his sub-commanders at the farthest end of the long table from Ambrosius, as the leaders dined that evening in Kinarius's hall. Hounds waited by the hearth for bones to be thrown to them, and servants scurried back and forth from the kitchens with food and drink. The mood was sombre as all knew of the royal spat.

Verica turned to Brian and whispered, "Word has got out and there is much support for Uther's proposal. Even I would welcome an opportunity to return to my lands and check on their security."

"Aye," Brian replied, "I also feel we should be seen in our lands. There are many still working the fields who would be comforted by our presence. But how to do we broach the subject?"

"I fear Ambrosius is fixated on making a base from which he will hunt down Vortigern, or at least raid his lands. Perhaps we should talk to him in the morning, for his sour mood has been worsened by wine."

A HAWK FELL through the blue sky, twisting and turning until it struck a starling, scattering the flock. Vortigern watched through the bars of his window, high up in the tower of his palace in Camulodinum. Beyond was the sea, with wooden ships sailing up the estuary on their way to trade at Londinium.

"We must escape and flee west to our lands," he said, turning to face his fellow captive.

"But how, Father?" the thin youth replied from his slumped position.

"I named you after my noble brother in the vague hope that some of his wisdom would rub off on you," Vortigern moaned. "There must be some servants in this place who would carry a message to the outside and help us get out of this mire of Saxon scum!"

Vortimer looked up. "The boy who brings our meals is known to me..."

"Well, why did you not say that before!" his father stormed. "I will write him a note to convey to... whom? I know not who could help us."

"Maybe he could take it to the port and look for your captain?" Vortimer offered helpfully.

The Emperor of Britannia stroked his beard and thought. "You might just have something there. Perhaps you do have some of your late uncle's brains after all. Yes, Pericles may still be plying his trade between the island and the port. I will write a note to him and you talk to the boy. He must hide the note in his jerkin and not speak of this to anyone."

The youth beamed with joy at the rare praise from his father, and at the thought that they were hatching a daring escape plan.

AMBROSIUS SAT IMPASSIVELY on Perseus, who pawed impatiently at the dusty earth. He was not happy that he had been persuaded to back down, but the weight of opinion from his commanders was stacked against him. Uther, Verica and Drustan had departed to ride east with some six hundred mounted cavalry, whilst Constans, Tomos and the remaining troops, together with those of Kinarius, prepared to travel north with their king.

Brian remained with his family and a small group of soldiers, to wait for the order to follow on with the Atrebates. Ambrosius had been forced to learn a lesson; that it was prudent to consult before making snap decisions, or risk losing the backing of his supporters. Kinarius had further irked him by strongly advising that they should leave the Atrebates tribe behind. They would send for them once a deal had been brokered with those living in and around Corinium. To dispossess its citizens by force would not endear him to his supporters, and make him look no better than the hated Saxons.

"The circlet on my head is as thin as a beggar's gruel," he muttered to Tomos.

"My lord, the people see you as a great king and a source of hope in uncertain times," his deputy replied.

Ambrosius managed a smile and his mood lightened a little. "With the loyalty of fearless warriors like you about me, Tomos, I feel invincible!" An idea was already forming in his head as he spurred his stallion forward. "Advance!" he yelled, forcing the unprepared Kinarius to hurriedly mount and follow.

THE SOUND OF Saxon war drums carried on the wind, causing Vortigern to glance over his shoulder as he shinned down a rope that had been smuggled in by the boy. Valorian followed and they leapt on horses brought by Captain Pericles, riding by moonlight into the forest to the north. Pericles handed them over to the sons of Gorbonuc of the Trinovantes, and they were guided beyond the settlements now occupied by growing numbers of Germanic people, who called themselves Angles.

"They are the Angliscs, or 'English' in our way of saying," a young chief explained as they dismounted at a farmhouse in a remote clearing. Vortigern was handed on to a nervous farmer for the remainder of the night.

"My thanks to you brave lads. I see the likeness in your faces of your noble father, so cruelly slain at my table by those treacherous Saxon dogs and that bitch they married me to. I will be back with an army, so await my call and raise your people in revolt on my command."

With that they departed, leaving their emperor and his son to eat porridge with a lowly farmer and his awe-struck family. Gone was the crown and purple cloak, but not the steely determination in his eye.

8. Hope in the West

SOMETHING GLINTED IN the distance. Sunlight on metal, perhaps? A spear tip or helmet, flashing through the leaves. The ground beneath them trembled. A telltale puff of dust preceded the sound of jangling bits mixed with deep male voices as birds took to the sky.

"My lord, riders approach! Saxons!" a scout gasped, as Uther, Verica and Drustan sat impassively on their mounts. They were on a small hillock in the western part of the kingdom of Ceint, slightly above a large meadow of long grass and patchy gorse, with no more than a dozen mounted soldiers at their back.

"Fall into line and let's wait," Uther growled. In a matter in minutes a wave of riders burst out of the greenery on the far side of the meadow, high grass and rusty flower stems separating the two groups at barely one hundred paces. The Saxon front line fanned out before them until over fifty riders had entered the meadow. They stopped and faced the Britons, their conical helmets and spear tips glinting in the morning sun.

"Remember the plan," Verica shouted, reining his horse. "Act startled and bolt!"

Uther and Verica turned to their right, Drustan to his left, and led their troops at a fast gallop away from the meadow, following paths beneath overhanging trees. The Saxons let out a battle cry and charged across the meadow, their horses prancing over the knee-high grass. Some peeled off to chase after Drustan and his smaller troop of Belgaic warriors.

Uther and Verica raced along a path beside a rippling stream, following its snaking course as it narrowed and rose towards its source. The flood plain gave way to a narrow valley, with gently rising slopes of bush-scrub and small trees getting steeper and higher. The path darkened when overhanging trees crowded in on the riders, who pressed their mounts onwards and upwards, aware that they were being pursued. They burst out of the woods into bright sunlight and were forced to shield their eyes.

A group of fifty or more mounted archers awaited them, and they turned their mounts in front of the group to face the path. Below, they heard the pounding rhythm of charging horses, and seconds later the first Saxon riders emerged out of the woods.

"Fire!" Uther yelled, and a hail of arrows rained down on the first dozen or so warriors. Another volley of arrows felled half a dozen riders and pierced the flanks of terrified horses that reared up, dismounting their riders.

"Charge!" yelled Uther and they advanced on the milling Saxon riders, some still partially blinded by the sunlight. The cavalry soldiers had stowed their bows and now gripped javelins in their throwing hand as they approached the enemy at a canter. Javelins arced through the air, striking down with deadly effect on their screaming enemy. Uther and Verica entered the fray, slashing about them with their broadswords.

Further down the path a skirmish raged; Drustan had executed a devastating ambush on their rear ranks. Uther recognised the Saxon leader, a large fierce man wielding a huge double-edged axe. It was Horsa, brother of Hengist. Uther was distracted by a sword swipe, and he lost sight of the Saxon leader as he duelled with a horseman. Horsa, seeing Verica's noble attire, spurred his horse towards him, coming at him from behind as he exchanged blows with another Briton.

With a thunderous cry, he brought down his axe on Verica's helmet, splitting it in two, the blade lodging in the top of his head. Verica rolled in his saddle; his sword fell from his hand, and slowly he tumbled from his mount, the axe handle protruding from his mop of dark curly hair.

Horsa celebrated with whoops as Briton eyes turned in anguish at the sight. The Saxons were encouraged by their leader's defiance and hammered harder at their foes with axe and sword. Uther yelled his rage and kicked his horse forward, making straight for the huge Saxon. Horsa saw him coming and laughed as he drew his sword. They clashed with a deafening sound of metal on metal, and menaced each other, looking for a chance to strike. Uther lunged at Horsa, grazing his arm and drawing blood. The Saxon yelled and rode straight at him, causing both their horses to stagger, dismounting them both. They circled each other as the fighting raged around them, gripping their swords in both hands. The stocky Uther was considered a big man by his peers, but Horsa towered over him, standing over six feet in height. Blows were aimed and parried as they looked for a strike to disable their opponent.

Horsa's red eyes were wide with rage and pain, and he sought a swift ending to the match. He took a run at Uther, swinging his sword from above his head, looking for a decisive blow. Uther dodged to his right and stuck out a leg, tripping the charging warrior. Horsa fell, and Uther was upon him, thrusting the point of his sword, through the thick layers of hide and fur, into the side of the Saxon leader. Horsa roared his pain and tried to roll away. Uther withdrew his blade and swung it down at his enemy's head, but Horsa managed to raise his sword to parry the blow. Uther circled him, knowing he was fatally wounded, but still dangerous. The giant Saxon tried to stand up, and Uther saw his chance, delivering a blow that half severed the head of the groaning man.

Horsa was dead. A groggy Uther was helped to his mount to see his men overcome the remaining Saxons, slaughtering all those who did not flee. Before long, Drustan and his surviving soldiers emerged from the forest path. He and Uther dismounted and stood in silence as they looked down on the bloody remains of Verica.

"Such misery I feel at this sight! We have won our victory," moaned Drustan, "but at what cost? The wise and much-loved Verica will be sorely missed."

Uther replied, "Aye, he was a friend and a good commander. We shall take his body to his longhouse. It is but a day's ride from here. What is the name of this place?"

Drustan consulted with his men before replying. "They say the settlement by the river is called Epps Ford, my lord."

"Then we have defeated the Saxons this day, slaying mighty Horsa, and have won our battle at Epps Ford," Uther said. "Let us bury our dead and bind noble Verica's body. Count the number of Saxons slain and bring me the head of Horsa in a sack, along with his sword, arm bands and torque, as proof of his death. It is a painful price to pay for our trophies."

It took two men to remove the axe blade from Verica's head, such was the force that had planted it there. Uther and Drustan invoked the spirits of their tribal gods as they paid homage to their fallen men around their burial mound. The Saxon dead were left for the locals to find and strip of their clothing.

"THEY ARE EVEN taking the cobblestones from the roads," Constans moaned, as they slowly made their way some thirty miles north to the former Roman legionary garrison town of Corinium.

Ambrosius replied, "Aye, all is being looted and it seems there are few tradesmen to make things. Without the Romans to drive the locals, they have reverted to barbaric ways."

Kinarius heard and said, "My people are free from Roman slavery, my king, but I see the slow decay of what was once important to Rome, and less so to us."

Ambrosius turned to him and replied sourly, "My noble Kinarius, for how long will you use the bathhouse, and live in the magistrate's house behind the stone walls of Aqua Sulis, watching it all fall about you? And surely you can see that these roads are useful for travel?"

"Aye, my lord," he replied, "but they were built by an invading army, for their own purposes. I agree we make use of the Roman buildings, but already the people are drifting back to village life. They must grow crops and keep pigs to survive. So, we go back to our ways, and the buildings of Rome crumble or provide stone and timber for more modest abodes. To us, it is no longer Aqua Sulis, but Caer Badon. Minerva and the Roman gods have left with the legions, and our river goddess, Sulis, remains."

Their talk was interrupted by returning scouts. "My lord! Settlement ahead, some two miles."

"Any sign of soldiers?" Constans asked.

"None, my lord."

The villagers were startled by the approaching riders and many ran to hide. Ambrosius and the chief entered a flimsy stockade and stopped outside a simple barn. Kinarius dismounted and went inside. Before long he reappeared with three men.

"My lord Ambrosius, this is Darius, the village headman, and his sons."

"Hail Darius," Ambrosius said, dismounting. "Pray tell, who is the lord of these lands?"

"Hail mighty king, we have heard of your battle with Emperor Vortigern, who rules these lands. Our chief is Morvidius, who dwells in Corinium."

"And how far is that place?"

"My lord, in just another three miles you will see the Roman walls."

Kinarius added, "He tells me this Morvidius is a kinsman of Vortigern, and so we should not expect a welcome there."

"Indeed. Then let us ride swiftly and find out. Good day to you, Darius!" Ambrosius jumped back on Perseus and led them out of the stockade and into a canter along the road to Corinium.

The Romans had cleared the land around the walled town, as was their way, for one hundred paces in all directions. Now, the advancing force cleared the tree line and found themselves surrounded by a shanty village of crude shacks and pig pens, with grubby children and chickens picking at the muddy soil. Villagers bent over rows of cabbages and other root vegetables stood to stare in silence at the coloured pennants on the warriors' lances.

Ambrosius had expected to see the gates of the town closed to them, but saw they were open. Constans stopped them short of the walls and said, "My brother, there may be an ambush within. Send an advance party to clear our way to the chief's hall."

"Very well, but not you, dear brother. Remain here with me."

"I shall go," said Kinarius.

"Then take my guard to accompany you, and my impersonator, Tomos," Ambrosius replied, passing his crowned helmet to his trusted deputy.

A dozen riders entered through the stone gatehouse whilst the remaining group of two hundred waited outside. Children approached the impassive warriors and begged for coins. An eerie quiet descended on them, disturbed only by the champing on bits and snorting of the horses. Stony sentries stared from the gatehouse parapet and lolled indolently from the defensive walls. After ten minutes, Kinarius appeared at the gate and waved them in.

Constans, ever cautious, rode at the head of the troop, accompanied by Tomos, having persuaded Ambrosius to hang back. They passed across a wooden bridge and through the gatehouse, into a wide courtyard, and fanned out on either side to form two rows of riders. Across the yard, at a distance of thirty paces, a line of sixty or more black-clad mounted soldiers faced them. Behind were men-at-arms with long lances and archers lined the walls above.

Constans, Kinarius and Tomos cautiously crossed the courtyard and stopped before the large double doors of an imposing stone building. Moments later, the doors were pushed open by two guards. A black-bearded man, of average build, appeared on the stone terrace, wearing a long, bleached gown bordered and belted with gold silk. His hands were hidden in his sleeves.

Kinarius spoke first. "Hail, cousin Morvidius! Greetings to you. I present Ambrosius Aurelianus, Roman tribune and now proclaimed king of the Britons by the Council of Chiefs, and his noble brother, Constans! We ask for your welcome and hospitality in your hall."

His words were greeted by a tense silence as Morvidius shifted his stare from Kinarius to Constans before falling on a stern-faced Tomos.

"You are welcome, Cousin Kinarius. But you bring with you a rebel army led by a usurper to the throne of my kinsman, Emperor Vortigern." Morvidius's words were a clear challenge, and hands moved to sword hilts. After enjoying the moment, he broke into a broad smile.

"Ha ha! Please come. Let your 'king' and his commanders enter my hall and we shall talk over a cup of sweet mead. Men-at-arms, stand down! There will be no fighting here." His soldiers lowered their weapons and some tension was released.

The line of mounted guards moved away, returning to their stables in the barrack enclosure to one side of the square-enclosed town. It was slightly bigger than Calleva, Ambrosius noted, fitting its description as a major base for the legion's forays to the west and north of the island. He rode forwards, still anonymous amongst his sub-commanders, and dismounted before entering the great hall to join Tomos and Kinarius.

"You are welcome!" Morvidius boomed across the dimly lit room. "Come forward and sit around my table. This place was once the magistrate's court where justice was dispensed in Roman times. Now it is my hall where all business and rulings are made. Come forward."

They sat around his banquet table and were served with mead in pewter beakers and flat bread on trays. Ambrosius, sitting with his men, shook his brown curls as he took off his helmet. He may have been wearing the helmet of a humble cavalry soldier, but it was clear for all to see that he had the bearing of a leader.

Morvidius took his seat at the head of the table, and beckoned to Kinarius, Tomos and Constans to sit beside him.

"My dear Kinarius," he said. "Do you think I would fall for your deception? This noble to my left is not Ambrosius. Pray, make the correct introductions."

Kinarius stood and said, "My noble cousin, it was but an act of caution merited by any approach to unknown territory. Let me introduce you to Prince Constans of Amorica, and Tomos of Gaul, a noble commander." The two men nodded to their host. "And in the middle of his commanders, may I introduce Ambrosius Aurelianus, King of the Britons."

Ambrosius stood and bowed slightly. "I thank you for your welcome, Chief Morvidius."

Morvidius regarded him, stroking his black beard. "My uncle, Vortigern, would castigate me for such a welcome. But the news has reached us, as I am sure it has reached you, of his imprisonment by the Saxons who have seized control of his court and murdered his loyal followers. This, along with news of your victory over his army in battle, well, changes things..."

His voice tailed off as if he could think of nothing to add. They drank in awkward silence until Ambrosius rose to his feet again.

"Noble Morvidius, the kings and chiefs of the south and western parts of this island have seen need to appoint me as their champion, as they fear the spread of the Saxons through the land. Now we have seen a clear sign of their intentions. Do you agree with us that all Britons who value their peace and security must stand together to resist them? Vortigern has made an error by employing them to fight for him, for they see their chance to settle here. They are looking past him to covet your green fields. Let us not see each other as enemies, I beseech you." His men banged their beakers on the table in raucous support as he took his seat.

Morvidius laughed and said, "I cannot fault your argument, sir. But whilst my lord and king, Vortigern, lives, I cannot swear allegiance to any other. Yet, as you say, it is unproductive for us to fight; soon the Saxons may come, and we must be ready to resist them. Yes, it is a time of great uncertainty in this land." He raised his voice across the table. "Come, let us eat."

Serving boys and girls brought meat and vegetables from the kitchen, and they ate with relish. It was going well for Ambrosius, but his mind was on the thorny subject of settlement. Morvidius had given no indication that he knew of their plans to take over the town.

He whispered to Kinarius, "I will need your wise council on how to take over this town from your kinsman. Remember, I am building my kingdom here, and you, my friend, shall be one of my commanders and shall profit as a consequence."

Kinarius smiled and replied, "My lord, you have already proved yourself in battle, and I know you will be a strong and powerful ruler who will bring security to my people and these lands. My sword is yours."

Ambrosius needed to act soon; the smiling Kinarius was no tested ally, no Verica, and he should not be given the opportunity for betrayal. "Stay by me," he said, "and together with Constans we shall speak to our host after this meal."

UTHER AND DRUSTAN were as good as their word. They swept along the south coast, through ports and settlements, attacking and slaying what few Jutes they encountered on the way to Noviomagus and Verica's fortified village. There they recounted the story of the Battle of Epps Ford, and how noble Verica had died, fighting valiantly against a Saxon army, and how Uther had avenged Verica by killing the Saxon chief, Horsa. Preparations were made for a Christian burial, as was desired by his kinsfolk. There was no widow, nor children, and the succession of Chief of the Regnii would now pass to a trembling younger brother, Knut.

"Young Knut, we will support you," Drustan said, putting his arm around the grieving youth.

"My thanks, my lord," he mumbled.

"And what of his pair of fine hunting dogs?" Uther asked, rubbing the heads of the mournful wolfhounds. "I would like to present them to our king, Ambrosius. What say you?"

The young man could not refuse the hulking warrior who stood before him. "Please take them, and my pledge of loyalty, to your master," he stammered.

MORVIDIUS TOOK HIS guests to the top of the tower at the back of the hall.

"From here we can see over the town and the fields beyond the walls," he said with a sweeping wave of the arm. Ambrosius noted that the walls were largely intact, although there were some gaps where stone blocks had been removed. Morvidius followed his gaze and said, "Ah yes, on that side of town, next to where the tradesmen and traders are quartered, they have taken away some stones and made a pathway over the rubble to a dumping ground for waste outside the walls. Indeed, part of the moat on that side is now full of putrid human waste and rotting remains of animals. It has a foul smell that oft drifts to us when the wind is from the east."

Ambrosius grunted and looked to the west, where the legions would have been barracked.

"Over there is the barrack blocks, some in use by my soldiers, and some for married quarters. Next to it is the coliseum, disused and now the home to beggars and unfortunates."

Ambrosius asked, "And how many guards do you have, noble Morvidius?"

"You have seen them," he replied. "Fifty mounted cavalry and one hundred gatekeepers and guards. We have four gatehouses, although only two are in regular use."

"It is a town falling into disrepair," Constans said, pointing to the houses below. "Look where the thatch has crumbled and building walls are falling."

Morvidius bridled and replied, "Noble lord, we maintain what we need, and have only three hundred souls now living in the town. Many have drifted away to farming settlements, whereas the old nobility have crossed the sea to Amorica where it is said there is fine living."

Constans and Ambrosius shared a laugh at this comment.

"And what is the cause of your mirth, my lords?" Morvidius said, somewhat tersely.

"I am sorry, my lord," Ambrosius laughed, clutching the chief's shoulder. "We laugh because we are from Amorica and now, because of your compliment, miss our fine life there more than ever! It is true that many nobles who cling to the Roman ways have moved to the land of our uncle, King Aldrien."

They had finished surveying the town and Ambrosius had all the information he needed.

"My noble Morvidius," he said, with his hand still on the shorter man's shoulder, "I must tell you now that I intend to take up residence in your town and base my army and my followers here."

He had locked his eyes on the startled man, who tried to pull himself free of his grip. "But, you cannot just take my town! I am holding this area for my lord Vortigern..."

"Who has been deposed by the Saxons," Ambrosius interrupted. "This town suits my purpose and I will restore it and make it a fortress once again. I invite you to remain with me, as the town clerk, and also your people, whom I will not remove. We shall rebuild the barracks and the town houses to make accommodation for new arrivals. This will happen, my lord, with or without your support. So what say you?"

"My lord Kinarius!" he squeaked.

Kinarius shrugged and said, "I have seen the army commanded by King Ambrosius, only part of which is here, and have sworn my allegiance to him. Under his banner, we can become a strong nation again and resist the invaders who trouble our lands. I say, you would be wise to accept his offer to remain and manage the affairs of the town."

The squirming man was more accountant than soldier; that much was plain. Surrounded by three tall warriors, he could do little else but submit.

"So be it," Ambrosius said, as his unhappy host nodded his assent. "In the morning, you shall announce to the townsfolk

and your guards that I am the new ruler of Corinium, and the
mounted guards will become part of our cavalry regiment.
Good! Let us retire to my hall to toast our union with my best
wine!"

SIX RIDERS APPROACHED the gatehouse of a wooden
stockade as the sun set before them.

"Halt! Who approaches?" a guard shouted from the parapet.

"We come in peace!" a hunched man replied, removing his
hood to reveal his grey hair.

"State your business!" the guard shouted, as more men came
running to his side. Two other riders came forward and
removed their cowls.

A well-built man with grey-flecked black hair and beard
shouted up, "I am your king and emperor, Vortigern! Open the
gates!"

Squinting in the half-light at the ragged group, the guard
was unsure what to do. The only previous time he had seen the
Emperor Vortigern, some nine months earlier, he had ridden
out of these gates with his escort, riding a magnificent horse,
wearing a cloak of purple and a golden crown on a well-
groomed head. After a moment's hesitation, he shouted back,
"Hold fast! The Captain of the Watch is coming!"

Amid much commotion, a man in armour appeared and
leant over the parapet holding a burning torch above his head.
"Who goes there?" he shouted at the huddled group below.

"I am Vortigern, your emperor! Open the gates or I will flay
you alive!" The voice was familiar to the captain who ordered
the gates be opened. He hurried down the wooden ladder to see
for himself and confirm the identity of the modest rider,
wrapped in a grey woolen cloak. He took hold of the bridle of

the horse and, looking up, recognised the worn features of Vortigern.

"Apologies, my lord! I now see it is you! Welcome to your fortress home, Genoreu!"

"Yes, yes," Vortigern replied, leaning forward on his horse. "I have escaped from the Saxons and now return to my birthplace for comfort and solace! Pray look after my guides in the hostel, and escort Prince Vortimer and myself to my hall!"

9. A New Order

"THERE IS NEVER a good time for bad news, Brother," Constans said, the thick fog of his words melting into the cold air. He awkwardly flexed his healing arm as he looked over the battlements at the tree line beyond the town of Corinium.

"Aye, but you add to my misery by announcing you wish to leave," Ambrosius replied, mournfully.

Constans turned to study the busy scene below: carpenters and tradesmen jostling in the street, the good-natured shouts of men with purpose.

"The news of the death of our dear uncle, King Aldrien, was accompanied by a request for us to return to Amorica to be part of the resolution. You have reason to stay here in Britannia, to consolidate your new kingdom, but I, on the other hand, feel my place is back home, in the mire of politics about the corpse of our illustrious uncle. I beseech you, give me your blessing to depart, and allow me to take the Amorican auxilliaries who have served you so loyally."

Ambrosius wrapped his cloak about him to keep out the cold and looked balefully at his brother.

"You have been at my right hand since this adventure began, dear Constans. And now I must do without you. Yes, of course you must go, and report there of our deeds in this wet and windy island. Amorica must remain our ally. Our soldiers have served us well these past four years, and must be yearning to see their friends and families. With the exception of my most trusted bodyguards, take them, but be sure to keep your sub-commanders close to you. There may be danger from our cousins who might see you as a threat. Tread carefully, my dear brother; speak well of me, and go with my blessing."

Tomos and Regan huddled together for warmth under his red woollen cloak, sheltering in a kitchen doorway at the back of the hall. An outbreak of plague in Corinium had afflicted her brother, Patch, and she was tired from nursing him.

"My love," she said, "can you speak to the Lady Cordelia for a remedy for his fever?"

"Of course I will. And I will take you to her to request a position for you. Your experience as a waiting girl in the tavern in Calleva could best be described as... a personal attendant."

He smiled and kissed her lightly on the cheek, pulling her closer to him, as they reverted to staring at the pools of muddy water in the courtyard. Tomos had taken Regan as his wife, and had moved both her and Patch into his tiny officer's quarters.

She could sense his restlessness. "I know you hate being confined by these walls and yearn to be marching to war with your soldiers," she said, squeezing his hand.

He smiled at her as he replied, "That is where I feel most useful and at ease. Fighting and killing men are the things I am most skilled at; but now I bear the rank of centurion; I have the responsibility of organising and leading my unit. Yes, I love you and am happy to have you by my side, but I cannot deny that my mind is fixed on putting my men through a tough route march in the morning, regardless of the weather."

The grey drizzle formed a sheet in front of the two lovers, content, for now, to enjoy the silence.

Ambrosius had been busy establishing his command and organising building works. This was hampered by the early onset of winter and the outbreak of a mysterious fever that had afflicted many in the town, covering their bodies in rashes and causing delirium. Added to this, his mother, Cordelia, was unwell.

"I'm just tired," she had said. "I'm an old woman who has lost her husband and been dragged across the country! Let me rest." He regularly visited her and his caring sister, Esther.

"Dear Mother, you look much better today," he quipped, presenting Esther with a bowl of dried fruit.

"My son, you flatter me," she said, smiling weakly. "We both know there is no cure for old age."

"Only the gods know the day of your ending," he said.

"Let me correct you, my son," she said, coughing before continuing. "The one true God knows the time when He will receive my soul. On that matter, please send Father Andreus to me."

"I will send him if you drink that milk and eat some fruit. But your time is some way off, I am sure of it." He smiled at Cordelia, but his shoulders drooped as soon as he was out of her chamber.

He would throw himself into supervising the building works and the successful meshing of the local warriors with his own men. Many of the Atrebates tribe had been housed outside the town walls in temporary huts, waiting to be allocated housing within. They seemed to have been spared the plague, and he was keen to keep them out of the town until the sickness abated. The sickness must be passed from the afflicted to those who come into close contact with them. He had seen this before, and knew the solution was to quarantine the part of town where it was most prevalent. This he would do now, and have strict control of entry and exit, with guards set day and night.

The following day, a page hurried into the great hall to announce riders approaching. Ambrosius ordered the guards to man the gates and walls and went to the parapet over the gatehouse to see for himself who approached. Brian joined him and they looked out together over the tree line at the gathering dust cloud.

"Where is Tomos?" he asked.

Brian summoned a guard and asked, "Well? Where is he?"

"My lord, he is without, running in the woods with his men," came the reply.

"Who is the captain of the guard?" Brian demanded, tetchily.

Kay came running to him. "It is I, my lord," he blurted, tucking his leather jerkin into his sword belt.

"Then get your men to stand ready!" Ambrosius thundered.

The oncoming grey haze indicated a sizable number of riders approaching from the south. Ambrosius strained his eyes as the banners came into view.

"It's the dragon banner of Uther!" he shouted, slapping Brian on the back. "And the noble Verica! At last, some good news! Let us prepare a welcome feast!"

They hurried to the high-beamed governor's hall where Ambrosius ordered all his attendants, including the town clerk, Morvidius, to be present when he greeted the returning heroes of the eastern expedition. All thoughts of his angry stand-off with Uther were long forgotten, as the fearless warrior instincts of his brother were secretly admired and much valued.

"Ah-ha! My dear brother returns!" he said, as he pushed himself off his throne and strode forward to embrace Uther. His brother's eyes gleamed, but there was something there. Was it regret or sadness in his silent smile? "Well met, Lord Uther, I am pleased to see your safe return, and with these two fine hunting hounds."

"I have found you at last, dear Brother!" Uther boomed, slapping the king on the back, as no other would dare to do. "We looked for you at Aqua Sulis and were directed here."

Ambrosius scratched the head of the large wolfhounds and said, "I remember these two, and the part they played in saving my life from Jutish assassins. Come, sit next to me and tell me of your deeds. But where is my dear friend, Verica?"

He cast his eyes over the group of dusty warriors, huddled together in the centre of the room. "Where is Verica?" he demanded, in a louder voice.

Uther took his arm and said, "My lord and brother, I bring bad tidings of the noble Verica. He was slain in battle with the Saxons at a place called Epps Ford..."

"What!" Ambrosius pulled free of him and staggered, incredulous, his face draining of blood. "How can he...? The most noble of chiefs, gone!"

He sat heavily on his throne, head in hands. Those present looked uncomfortable to witness his grief. There had been sorrow at the loss of Marcus, but this reaction was more nakedly emotional.

"I have brought you Lord Verica's two favourite hunting dogs," Uther offered weakly, as he moved nearer to his distraught brother. He had never before thought on the closeness of the bond between Ambrosius and Verica.

Uther signalled an attendant to bring drinks, and after some time, he told the story of the battle. Drustan stepped forward holding a hessian sack.

"We took trophies of the Saxon chief, Horsa, the brother of Hengist. He is surely a big loss to the Saxon cause." He nodded to Drustan who rolled a grizzly head onto the stone floor. Uther knelt as he presented Horsa's sword and gold armband to Ambrosius, who held the two objects in his hands, turning them over as if they were strange and unknown treasures.

Finally, he spoke. "It is a great and noble victory, my brother, and noble Drustan; I salute you and your men. The slaying of a Saxon chief is a blow to our enemy and shows our defiance of their aggressive intent on our island. We will talk later at your welcome feast. Tomos, show our noble warriors to their quarters." They all withdrew, the anguish of their king depressing what should have been a celebration at their triumphant return.

"Warriors die in battle," Uther remarked to Tomos as they filed out of the hall. "That is understood and accepted. My brother's grief is excessive. We will salute our fallen, in our usual manner, this eve at the feast."

"He mourns not just for his fallen friend," Tomos said in a low voice, "but also for the loss of his brother Constans, who has returned to Amorica with three hundred of the Amorican auxilliaries. There remains just myself and thirty of our men to form his personal escort."

Uther stopped and stared at him. "How did this parting happen?"

Tomos replied, "News came of the death of their uncle, King Aldrien, and Constans requested to go there."

"My brother is soft in the head to allow his Amorican auxilliaries to depart. We lack skilled and experienced warriors. This leaves only his cohort of Roman legionaries."

"Aye," nodded Tomos, "but he gave leave for some of those to depart, to be with their families in Gaul. We now have just three hundred trained legionaries remaining, together with my thirty personal escort."

"This is not good. We must look to reorganise our rabble of warriors," Uther growled.

"I have an idea; I will propose it to our king once he is right-minded," Tomos replied. The two men clasped forearms and marched Uther's men to the barracks.

"My son, come closer," Cordelia whispered in a thin, cracked voice.

Father Andreus, her physician, and her maid hovered close by as Ambrosius bent forward on his stool, putting his ear close to her cracked lips. Esther and Brian, Uther and his frail wife, Jessica, barely containing the wriggling Morgana, leaned forward to try to hear.

"It is my dying wish that you find a suitable bride," she croaked. "A king must be married and provide for his succession. It is what Marcus would have wanted..." Her voice tailed off as she fell into sleep.

"Attend to her," Ambrosius said, sitting back in brooding silence.

Uther and Brian exchanged knowing looks. The physician fussed and the priest prayed as a respectful hush fell on the family. Ambrosius was about to get up when Cordelia opened her eyes. She looked past Ambrosius to Uther and beckoned to him with a bony hand.

"Come close, my son," she said. Ambrosius stood and Uther took his seat on the complaining stool, leaning forward uncomfortably to hear his mother.

"I prayed for your safe return, dear Uther," she said, flickering her eyelids as if fighting to stay awake. "You are my birth son and the heir to your father's name. I have prepared a document..." She coughed and her maid lifted her higher and adjusted the feather bolster. "A document, that sets out my will on the matter of inheritance." She looked at the priest who produced a rolled-up parchment.

"Father Andreus has borne witness to this and he is to convey the items listed therein to each of you. I have always treated all four of you as my children, and wish you all peace and happiness..."

Esther cried quietly as Cordelia slipped into her final sleep.

The Temple of Jupiter, a high-pointed stone building with a column-lined central courtyard, was now the Church of Saint Peter. Cordelia's funeral procession was escorted by a full guard of honour through the streets of Corinium, the route carefully avoiding the plague quarter. Ambrosius and Uther delivered a eulogy and a choir sang to ease the passage of her soul to Heaven. Ambrosius took in the scene and listened carefully to the sermon by Father Andreus. The words of his dear departed mother were in his head. He must move away from the worship of Roman gods and embrace the new Christian religion, for political reasons if not for faith. The influence of Rome was slipping away and a new order must be forged out of its ruin.

AMBROSIUS WAS POLISHING Excalibur in the peace of his chamber when Father Andreus knocked and entered on his command.

"My lord, I bring the items left to you from the lady Cordelia's will." He placed a large wooden box on a table, ornately carved and with bright jewels on the clasp.

Ambrosius opened the box and marvelled at the items within: Roman coins, arm clasps, a neck torque of fine silver and other bejewelled finery. There was a letter in Latin on parchment. Marcus had left him his memorabilia from the time of the Romans, but also some fine Celtic ornaments. In the letter, he repeated his desire for his son to combine the best of both worlds to make a new one, and unite the Briton tribes under one kingdom. Ambrosius smiled and tried on the wristbands, neck chain and torque.

This was how Tomos found him - in thoughtful mood but with a sad smile playing on his face.

"Ah, Tomos, come in and see what fine objects my parents have bequeathed me. Each one is bound to a memory," he added, in a low voice.

"My lord, they are wondrous to behold!" Tomos gushed, hoping to raise his master's spirits.

"And how are the men this fine morning?" he asked.

"My lord, the men are suitably accommodated and Lord Uther and Lord Brian await you orders. May I raise a matter with you, my lord, something that is on my mind?"

Ambrosius cocked an eyebrow at this unusually direct approach. "Of course, what is it?" he asked.

Tomos cleared his throat as if to make a speech. "My lord, with the balance of your army now heavily weighted towards Briton warriors, I wondered if the time was right to initiate a new rank of warrior... perhaps looking at other warrior nations for inspiration?"

"Tell me more, Tomos," Ambrosius said, with an indulgent smile. "Of which warrior tribes do you speak?"

"Well, my lord, the Germanic tribes have an order they call 'knights', who are a group of the best and most noble warriors in the land, who swear an oath of allegiance to their king."

"Ah yes, I have heard King Elafius mention this, and use of the term has already begun to sprout in certain places. Yes, I can see a need for this, to replace our old Roman ways and build something new, a new order of elite warriors, highly skilled and loyal. The men will look up to them and want to become like them." Tomos could see the sparkle return to his master's eyes.

"Yes, I see it now, they must be well-dressed and above the men, commanders who lead by example. Tomos, we must choose our valiant knights, and design a livery for them, so that all may know them."

Ambrosius was enthused by this notion, and immediately set about making a list. Tomos stood by his side.

"Perhaps our centurions shall become knights? What say you?" he asked, smiling.

Tomos saw his name at the top of the list. "My lord, I am deeply honoured…" he stammered.

"You shall be a knight, Tomos, and 'Sir' shall be your title. Now help me list our centurions and other nobles, but not royal princes. They remain above knights. In fact, I will list them separately." Ambrosius scratched on the parchment with his ink pen as Tomos threw suggestions at him. Before long, he sat back and admired his work.

"Before we have a ceremony, we must make up a livery for these knights – a singlet worn over their armour with my bear and dragon motif. Send Uther and Brian to me, and be sure to keep this a secret until our plans are set."

Tomos bowed and strode out. Ambrosius fingered the baubles in his box and formulated his plans. Winter was coming to an end, food stocks were low and the men were restless. Outside, the sound of laughter from the yard drifted through his window. It was time for action.

THE LAST SNOWS had melted and the warmer airs of spring brought more than birds and flowers, as the plague abated and the daily numbers of the dead and dying reduced to a mere handful. Ambrosius ordered the sluicing and scrubbing of the town's public places and issued an order that all dwellings and storehouses must be cleaned to drive out the large numbers of vermin. Since Ambrosius had made his court at Corinium, the sewage channels laid by the Romans had been restored, and the walls around the town repaired, with pits dug in the woods beyond by their Saxon and Briton slaves for waste to be buried.

He had received intelligence that Vortigern was in hiding at his fortress of Generou, close by Caer Gloui, only some twenty miles to the north and west. He was getting close to finalising his plans for a new order of knights, as a precursor to riding out to attack Vortigern, when a rider arrived in the town, announcing the imminent arrival of King Triphun and his attendants. Ambrosius was not expecting such a royal visit, and instantly reeled off a list of orders to prepare suitable accommodation and make ready for a feast.

"My royal brother! Well met!" Ambrosius awkwardly embraced the huge older man, who rumbled a deep throaty laugh, lighting up the hall with his presence.

"Young Ambrosius! High King of the Britons! I thank you for your welcome to your Roman town!"

Ambrosius laughed and guided his guests to sit at his long table. He bowed and kissed the hand of Queen Gweldyr, who was keen to introduce a young lady hovering behind her.

"My lord, this is our daughter, Gwendolyn, the Star of the West!"

Ambrosius bowed and kissed the hand of the beautiful strawberry-haired maiden, who fixed him with her beguiling green eyes. The queen's brother, Owain, and fellow distinguished military commander, Cadeyrn, he embraced warmly. Uther, Brian and Drustan were also boisterously reunited with their comrades from the Battle of Guloph, and laughter and merriment filled the hall.

Ambrosius sat next to Triphun and they fell into serious conversation about political matters, as the young men roared with laughter at the re-telling of key moments from the now-famous battle. Servants brought platters of food and jugs of mead, jugglers performed as dogs competed for scraps and bones. Triphun's normally cheerful face became grave as Ambrosius told him of the death of Verica and the battle to keep the Saxons at bay on the borders of Ceint. He became distracted and Ambrosius followed his gaze to the two Irish wolfhounds.

"Ah, yes. You may well recognise them as you gave them to Verica's father when they were pups. Uther brought them to me after Verica's burial. These dogs helped Verica and I fend-off Jutish assassins."

"Ah ha!" Triphun roared above the din. "I knew they were of my breeding stock! Loyal to their master, they will serve you well, my friend!" This lightened the mood and they ate and drank a while, enjoying the court jesters' tumbling, until Triphun leaned towards his host and said; "Do you find my fair daughter, Gwendolyn, appealing?"

Ambrosius was taken unawares and stammered, "My lord... I had not thought on the matter, indeed she is fair." He could see the gleam in the large Hibernian's green eyes and knew what was behind it. The words of Cordelia floated back into his mind, *a king must be married and provide for his succession.* He looked past Triphun to Queen Gweldyr and Gwendolyn and saw that they were both smiling at him. He welcomed the approach of Tomos who whispered in his ear, "My lord, we now have twelve tunics ready for your knights."

"Excellent, Tomos, all our knights are here so we shall have the ceremony tomorrow and then ride out to battle the day after. Go ahead and make the arrangements, and make use of Morvidius."

He turned back to Triphun, slightly more composed, taking a hesitant step towards the un-sprung trap of fate, and said, "Perhaps I could meet with the lady Gwendolyn and get to know her?"

"Ha ha!" Triphun boomed, standing and slapping Ambrosius on the back, "You have my blessing! Come, my daughter, and sit beside our king!" He leaned conspiratorially towards Ambrosius and whispered, "She comes with a handsome dowry including salt and silver mines."

A place was hurriedly set on the other side of Ambrosius and the young woman sat beside him. He knew he must look the opposite of how he felt – his stomach churned and his heart sagged - as all eyes were upon the couple and whispered conversations broke out around the hall. He leaned towards her, holding her hand and looking directly into her beautiful oval green eyes. Applause rang out around the hall, and the men whooped and cheered.

"My lord, you are blushing," Gwendolyn purred, as the trap door slammed shut.

Ambrosius touched the circlet on his head, settled it squarely. He pushed his chair back and stood, eying the raucous table until all eyes were on him and the room fell silent.

"I have a brief announcement to make," he said, pausing to gather his thoughts.

"Tomorrow, after noon, there will be a royal ceremony in this hall, where a new order of noble warriors, called Knights of the Dragon and Bear, will be unveiled. You shall all attend, so be mindful of sore heads!" Sniggers and murmurs ran around the table and he paused until they died down.

"This new order of knights will become the new commanders of our armies, and will include both men of common birth who have shown courage and leadership. Only kings and noble princes of the realm shall be above them. They shall be bound by an oath of honour and loyalty to their king. With this new order, we shall do away from the old structures of Roman legions and tribal warfare. We look to a new way of fighting and of conduct, to carry us forward into a new age where our island will be strong, well defended and united!"

Everyone jumped to their feet and roared their support, banging pewter mugs on the table and stamping their feet. Ambrosius looked with pride over the assembled nobles and nodded slowly. He held his hands up for silence.

"Pray continue your celebrations, but I will now retire to my preparations for the morrow. There will be no more announcements tonight!"

He bent and kissed the hand of Gwendolyn, slapped Triphun on the back, and indicated to Tomos and Morvidius to follow him. Guffaws and sniggers broke out as the guests were left with plenty to talk about.

TOMOS AND MORVIDIUS rose early and roused sleeping servants to begin cleaning the hall in advance of their dressing the walls with banners. The Lady Esther took charge of the kitchens, issuing instructions to a team of cooks and attendants. They were to prepare a feast and then garner rations for a marching army. Esther blessed the generosity of King Triphun who, in his wisdom, had brought cooks and supplies with him for his guard.

The pair next hastened to give prior warning to those who would be made knights, without giving detail of what was to take place: they must present themselves in their best appearance, wearing armour that had been cleaned and polished.

Ambrosius ordered the bells to be rung at noon and invited guests began to arrive at the hall. King Elafius arrived with some fifty guards and instantly sought out Ambrosius.

Most of the townsfolk gathered outside the building, the rumours of a celebration confirmed for them by the pageantry of the Royal Guard of thirty mounted soldiers parading in the square, their coloured pennants on long lances rippling in the breeze.

When the guests were seated, a trumpeter announced the arrival of the king, who entered with a sweep of his purple cloak, in full armour and finery – golden armbands at his wrists, a torque of silver around his neck, and a bejewelled crown of gold on his head. Ambrosius read from a parchment scroll.

"My fellow kings, Triphun of Dyfed and Elafius of Dumnonia; assembled lords and ladies; warriors and attendants, we are here today to initiate a new order, whose noble warriors shall be called the Knights of the Dragon and Bear."

Thunderous applause broke out amongst the intrigued gathering of close to one hundred, some of whom had little idea of what was to happen.

"This tradition we borrow from Germanic custom, and add our own distinct Briton flavour to it. From this day, the new commanders of our soldiers will be knights, so chosen for their proven military skills and loyalty to our cause. However, more than military experience is required of our knights. They must also uphold a code of honour and respect to all, thereby leading by example. This code shall include the following:

Never, without provocation, to assault or murder any person,

To swear loyalty to their king and country,

To show mercy to their enemies when defeated,

To be respectful and helpful to ladies,

To fight only for their king and not for personal gain or profit,

To uphold the values and beliefs of the Christian Church."

He stopped reading and looked up at the silent faces around him. He put down the scroll and spoke directly.

"This may sound an unusual code for a warrior to embrace, but I believe in it, and believe it is the right way for us to forge a new land where the innocent will be protected and our enemies vanquished. Our enemies are pagans who worship Woden and idols in the dark forests. We shall embrace the new faith, Christianity. Knights will lead by example, being kind and gentle in times of peace, and as fierce as a cornered bear in times of war."

Another pause as sporadic applause rang out around the hall. "And now to the list of names." He turned to Tomos who handed him another parchment. Murmurs spread around the room in anticipation.

Ambrosius cleared his throat. "This list contains both those of noble birth and commoners, but all are as one, as proven military commanders. Kings and tribal chiefs who form our council are of a higher ranking in our kingdom and therefore will not be knighted. My brother Uther is a royal prince and councillor, and is deemed by me to be above this position."

Looks and whispers were exchanged and one question was on each person's lips: was Uther now heir apparent?

Ambrosius cleared his throat and continued. "These noble knights will now step forward to be knighted by my sword, Excalibur, and receive their tunics. First, my loyal brother, Brian."

Knowing he was the adopted son of Marcus, and that Uther, the birth son, would always outrank him, Brian showed no indication of being slighted. He stepped before Ambrosius and knelt on one knee. Ambrosius touched him lightly on the shoulder with his shining blade, and then put a tunic over his head.

"Stand and be recognised, Sir Brian, Knight of the Dragon and Bear." Brian stood proudly and bowed to his king, then took his place against the back wall of the hall, before a tapestry depicting the royal arms, facing the gawping multitude beyond the long table. The ceremony continued with Ambrosius's commanders; Sir Tomos and Sir Kay; the centurions, Sir Bors; Sir Pelleas; Sir Brastius and Sir Bagdemagus.

He paused for a mouthful of wine. "From Dyfed, to our west, Sir Cadeyrn and Sir Owain; from Dumnonia, to our south, Sir Percival, Sir Tristan and Sir Drustan."

The twelve knights, their tunics fitted, lined up along the back wall of the hall, to be admired by the gathering. Ambrosius continued, "These are our first knights. Each knight will have a squire to attend to his needs, and take quarters here in Corinium. They will not, however, remain in quarters, but will ride out on missions and attend to their other duties. My lords, ladies and fellow Britons, I now present to you the twelve Knights of the Dragon and Bear!"

"GOD'S TEETH! I leave you to build me a tower and return to find a pile of rubble!" Vortigern raged.

"My lord, we followed your orders and built a tower of stone on the side of yonder mountain across the river," a harassed engineer spluttered, pointing to a west-facing window, "but in the morning when we returned it had collapsed. I know not why..."

"Silence!" Vortigern screamed, glaring at the shrinking man through narrow, malevolent eyes.

"If you know not why, then you are no longer any use to me. Take him away!"

Guards grabbed the crestfallen man by both arms and dragged him from the hall.

Vortigern cast his cold black eyes over the dozen or so silent subjects before him. His eye settled on a curious and unfamiliar individual standing at the back. He was a tall man of indeterminate age, his long, unkempt brown hair falling about a narrow face with keen, piercing grey eyes. He was dressed in the fashion of the druids, in a grey woollen smock that was belted and reached his ankles.

"You! Come forward!" Vortigern commanded. The group of courtiers parted and the unusual visitor stepped into the gap. He half-bowed in a non-committal fashion.

"My lord Vortigern, I am Myrddin Emrys, known in these parts as Merlin, a healer from Dyfed, beyond the mountains." He swept his arm in the same direction as the unfortunate builder.

"Why are you in my court, Merlin the Healer?" Vortigern demanded.

"My lord, I can tell you why your tower collapsed, not once but twice, both times happening at night."

"Oh, really?" Vortigern cocked an eyebrow. "Pray tell."

Merlin cleared his throat and carefully chose his words. "Beneath the rock on which they try to build, lies a pool buried deep below. In this pool sleep two dragons, one white and one red. They sleep during the day but awake at night to fight, shaking the rocky foundations of your tower and causing it to collapse."

Stunned silence was quickly followed by raucous laughter, led by Vortigern.

"This is a fine story, Merlin! Pray tell us, what signify these white and red dragons?"

Merlin's face was set in a serious expression as he replied, "My lord, the red dragon symbolises your Briton army, and the white dragon represents the Saxon enemy. They will continue to fight until one is the outright winner. Therefore, I propose that you build the tower elsewhere."

Vortigern glared at him with malice. "I know not whether to have you killed for your impudence, or take you to the site of the tower and put you in charge of my builders! Does not one of you have a suggestion?" he barked, turning on the silent, shuffling attendants.

Vortigern stroked his beard until he caught the eye of his son, Vortimer. "And what say you, my boy? Shall we believe this wandering shaman?"

Vortimer was fascinated by the calm and confident manner of the plain-speaking Merlin, who had addressed his father in a direct fashion seldom seen in his court of cowering flatterers.

"I shall be pleased to accompany Merlin, my father. I shall question him more closely on these battling dragons, and on the best location for your tower."

"Fine, let it be so," Vortigern said. "I am tired of this matter. But be warned, all of you. I will not accept any further excuses for failure. I want that tower built!"

10. A United Kingdom

THE GATES OF Caer Gloui remained stubbornly closed to Ambrosius and his army, who grazed their horses as they sat facing the wooden-fenced town. Vortigern's standard flew defiantly from above the gatehouse.

"I could blow a fart on that picket fence and it would fall down," Uther growled, keen for some action.

"Perhaps, my brother, but Vortigern is not within. Our scouts tell us he is in his fortress on a bluff above the river, some two miles beyond. That is where we shall go. We can deal with this unyielding town on our way back." He pulled on the reigns of Perseus and led his army westwards on a well-worn dirt track.

With Tomos's help, they had divided their army into twelve units, each under the leadership of one of the new knights. Countrymen fought together to promote inter-unit rivalry. Thus, Tomos's unit consisted almost entirely of former Roman soldiers and their Briton descendants, with their uniforms, shields and weapons reflecting this.

Other distinctive units included the Silurian cavalry, under Cadeyrn; the men of Dyfed, under Owain; the Belgae, under Drustan; the Dumnonians, under Percival; and the Men of Cournwall under Tristan. Other Briton tribes and foreign mercenaries were grouped under various knights, and Ambrosius encouraged them to display their banners and celebrate their unit identity. Units were partly mounted and partly on foot, each with their own supply wagons. With more men rallying to his call to battle, the army now stood at over six thousand.

They encountered no opposition and saw few locals as they made their way towards the fortress of Genoreu. The army emerged onto a plain, some five hundred paces in front of a part-stone and part-wooden stockade, surrounded by two rings of dry ditches with sharpened stakes protruding from the ground between them. A wooden drawbridge had been raised, completing the deep ditch before the fortress walls. Behind the fortress was a steep cliff above a wild, swirling river.

"There is but one way in and one way out," Ambrosius observed. "Have the men camp on this plain. We will talk to them in the morning."

Vortigern seethed with anger as he paced the parapet by torchlight. There was no way out, and they would be unable to survive a long siege if it came to that. The huge army outside, filling the plain with its tents and campfires, may well succeed in breeching their defenses. He had no allies to come to his aid. He was alone.

"First those damned Saxons and now this scrawny usurper! I should have killed the boy-child after finishing his father," he raged. "What are our options?" he demanded of a nervous captain.

"My lord, we have but two catapults to fire rocks and burning balls of pitch at them, and some two hundred archers. We have a further three hundred men-at-arms, who could throw javelins at an advancing army."

"It is a woeful report, Captain," Vortigern hissed through gritted teeth. "Send word to my family to prepare for escape. We are cornered here, like rats in a barrel."

A dawn drizzle soon lifted and a weak spring sun shone on the dewy grass as Ambrosius called his commanders to him. With Uther and twelve knights, it was now a sizeable committee.

"We shall ride forward and talk to the tyrant. The last time I faced him was before destroying his army at Guloph. This time I will finish him. He must not escape."

Uther grinned at the prospect. "My brother, this day has long been coming."

The Knights of the Dragon and Bear formed a protective shield in front of Ambrosius and Uther, as they approached the outer ditch before the gatehouse.

"These are pretty soldiers, Tribune Ambrosius," Vortigern shouted. "Once again you defy me with your rebellious rabble. I am still your king and emperor! Throw down your weapons and beg for my mercy. The Saxons are our true enemy!"

Uther sniggered and followed as Ambrosius urged Perseus forward beyond his knights.

"Yes, once again we face each other, Vortigern, and once again I will defeat you. Your wooden fences will not keep us out! Surrender now, and throw yourself on my mercy, and we shall spare your followers!"

Silence followed, and Ambrosius was happy for his words of dire warning to seep into the minds of Vortigern's terrified soldiers.

"An emperor does not surrender to rebels!" Vortigern shouted defiantly. He pointed to a trembling young man who had dropped his spear, and two burly guards grabbed the unfortunate youth by his arms. A cruel smirk played on Vortigern's face as he pointed to the stockade wall. The guards pitched him over the sharpened stakes and watched him tumble, screaming, to his death in the dry moat below.

Unimpressed, Ambrosius roared, "Then we shall come in and drag you out!"

He turned and led his men away.

Ambrosius and his commanders dismounted at his command tent to discuss their plan of action.

"We have one catapult, capable of firing bolts of iron at their gate until it breaks, but we need to bridge their moat."

Sir Bors, a Roman engineer, spoke. "My lord, we can build a bridge from these strong elm trees behind our position, but it will take half a day."

"Good, then take your men, and those you need from other units, Sir Bors, and start to build."

"I have seen their moat and have the measure of it, my lord; it shall be done." He bowed and left the tent.

Ambrosius turned to the restless Uther, "My noble brother, can you survey the cliff edge and see if they have an escape route? Place your men along the clifftop to ensure no one escapes."

"It shall be done," Uther said, bowing and leaving.

Expectant faces of men keen to do something surrounded Ambrosius. Sir Tomos stepped forward, puffing his chest out, now the equal of men he once thought his betters.

"My lord, may I speak?" He instinctively gave a Roman salute, beating his chest with clenched fist, drawing glares of disapproval from most of the Briton knights.

Ambrosius smiled, "Speak, Sir Tomos!"

"My lord, they appear few in number, and may cluster around the main gate, where our assault will be focused. Perhaps some of our archers should position themselves around the walls to left and right to keep their defenders busy and the walls guarded?"

Ambrosius beamed at his protégé, like a proud parent. "Yes, you are right, Sir Tomos. However, I want your men with me on the main assault on their gate. Sir Brian, take your archers to our left. Is there another unit with skilled archers?"

Sir Owain stepped forward. "My lords, the men of Dyfed are well practiced in the bow."

"So be it," Ambrosius replied. "Take your men to the right of our position, Sir Owain, and do what you can to keep the walls manned. The rest, with me, to plan our assault."

Their sole catapult was positioned in front of the main gates, at one hundred and fifty paces distance, just out of reach of their best archers. Reports that the elm bridge would soon be ready prompted Ambrosius to start the assault, with heated metal bolts loaded onto the machine and wound back by six men with wooden staves, retracting the rope to its full extent. The first bolt was fired and it arched through the air, hitting its target with a dull thud and a puff of black smoke. Cheers rang out from the troops, but as the smoke and dust settled, the gate was still in place. Further bolts were fired until, on the third hit, the crack of splitting wood rewarded them.

Engineers encouraged their men with shouts and threats to carry their wooden elm bridge forward, as the afternoon sun dipped towards the western mountains. The catapult fired more bolts while the helpless defenders looked on. On the impact of the fifth bolt, the gate finally started to collapse inwards.

Ambrosius gave the order and two lines of men hoisted up the bridge and moved forward, each protected from flying arrows by a comrade holding a shield above their heads. They tilted their platform upwards on its edge and let it fall forwards, until it slammed into position, forming a bridge over the moat. The men cheered again, as Tomos's well-drilled unit advanced, covered by rectangular shields at their front, sides and over their heads in a tight turtle formation.

As they approached the edge of their bridge, they were greeted with a flash of fire that singed their front shields and exposed ankles, causing their front rank to yell, 'halt!', as an intense heat engulfed them. Vortigern's men had poured pitch onto the elm bridge and set it alight with flaming arrows.

Tomos ordered his men to retreat, as fire roared on the bridge, but also set light to the damaged gate.

Both sides watched as the fire caught hold. The desperate occupants of the fortress tried to douse the flames on their gate to stop it spreading to their wooden ramparts. Ambrosius, seeing an opportunity to encourage the fire to spread, ordered Brian and Owain to pepper their walls and thatched houses beyond with flaming arrows.

For the next hour, Ambrosius and his men watched on as the fortifications and buildings within burned furiously. Yells and screams accompanied the scene of orange and yellow flames framed against a setting sun, as grey and black twists of smoke rose to the sky. The smaller huts and central long barn were now alight as the fire burned out of control. The death screams of animals joined those of the despairing multitude within the inferno.

"My lord!" Owain shouted as he rode to Ambrosius's position. "There is an attempt by some to escape the fortress by a concealed gate to the side. What are your orders?"

Ambrosius drew breath to reply above the din, but Father Andreus appeared by his side and forestalled him. "My lord, be mindful of your oath to be merciful to your enemies."

Ambrosius glared down at him. "Do not presume to force my hand, holy man. This is a field of battle, and I shall decide on their fate." Perseus stamped the ground and snorted loudly as Ambrosius reined him in.

"Sir Owain, instruct your men to help those who are trying to escape this inferno. We shall show mercy to our enemies, but I want Vortigern and his sons delivered to me, alive, or evidence of their deaths."

A stream of refugees flowed out of the rear of the burning fortress, as the gatehouse and wooden parapets collapsed into the flames.

"Build me another bridge!" Ambrosius shouted to Sir Bors. "Take the enemy nobles to the camp. I wish to question them. Give food and shelter to the people, but pen the soldiers and set a heavy guard."

Evening had set in and there was little else to be done except watch the bonfire die down to a smoldering heap, glowing orange against the night sky. Barely sixty had escaped. Genoreu was no more.

AMBROSIUS, UTHER AND a handful of knights sat on one side of a wooden table under a wide canvas awning. Before them stood a dozen nobles, their faces blackened by smoke, their hands and feet in chains of iron.

"Identify yourselves!" Uther roared in a loud voice that was not to be defied and made some jump.

A young man took a step forward and stood tall, trying to appear dignified as he surveyed the stony-faced men sat opposite.

"Sir, I am Vortimer, son of Vortigern. I humbly ask for your mercy, my lord, for myself and my followers."

"Your followers?" Ambrosius asked. "Where is your father, Vortigern?"

"He is dead, my lord, burnt in his long house. He refused to leave, my lord. It is the truth."

Ambrosius stared at him, wondering if it were true. "Pray, introduce your companions," he said after a short pause.

Vortimer identified two women close by him as his sister, Aylsa, and her handmaid. "And this is Merlin, a healer from Dyfed," he said, shifting attention to the end of the line where, in a singed grey smock, there stood a tall, long-haired man. "He is the one who led us out through a gate that had hitherto remained unseen and unknown to us. He has saved us from the inferno."

The victors looked at the gangly man of indeterminate age, who stared back with keen grey eyes that seemed to see into their heads. It appeared as if it were he who was regarding them.

"You have lied to us, young prince," Cadeyrn said, breaking the spell. "I know that the youngster there is your brother, Pascent." He pointed to the youngest member of the group, a forlorn looking boy with tousled blond hair. "I have seen you both riding behind your father."

"Is this so?" Ambrosius asked.

Looks were exchanged. "Yes, my lord," Vortimer replied in a low voice. "I wished to protect him from your vengeance, my lord. But I now also recognise Lord Cadeyrn who has attended my father's court, and fought at my father's side," he added with venom.

Ambrosius looked along the table at Cadeyrn and asked, "Are these two boys and this girl the only offspring of Vortigern?"

"Aye, my lord," came the reply.

All eyes were now on Ambrosius to hear his judgment on the captives.

After a lengthy pause, Ambrosius said, "No harm shall come to them. They shall remain under my protection at Corinium."

Uther glared at him, showing his displeasure. Ambrosius noted his look but ignored it. He turned back to the visibly relieved Vortimer.

"Young prince, will you guide my men to the place in the ruins where you last saw your father, and look for evidence of him? I would have his body identified; then we can accord him a Christian burial."

Vortimer nodded. Ambrosius needed proof of the tyrant's death to quash any claims that he had escaped, and to close a painful chapter in his life.

Vortigern's singed cloak, melted arm bands and crown were presented to Ambrosius, who authorized a simple grave be dug for his charred bones. Father Andreus said a few words, as Ambrosius sat impatiently on his horse behind the small group clustered around the grave. For once, his insensitivity was seen to rival that of Uther.

"Good riddance," Uther growled in his deep voice. "What orders, my brother?"

Ambrosius looked at him and replied, "I think your mind is on the town. Let us go there and I will show them these fire-damaged remnants of their emperor, and the young prince can bear testimony to his father's death and burial. Perhaps they will see sense and open their gates to us."

Uther ground his teeth and muttered, "This is a bloodless campaign."

"There will be Saxons aplenty to fight, Uther. Keep your sword sharp." With that, Ambrosius turned his horse and trotted away.

"And bring the young princes!" he shouted over his shoulder.

Prince Vortimer, barely seventeen years of age, felt the bitterness of loss and defeat as he was bounced along a rutted road in the back of a wagon. At least he was together with his younger brother and sister, their attendants, and the mysterious Merlin who had only recently come into their lives.

Ambrosius halted his army before the gates of Caer Gloui; those inhabitants who were kin to retired legionaries still called it Glouvia. It had once been an important Roman town, commanding the western borders with wild Dyfed and Silesia beyond a mighty river. He called the young prince to ride beside him, where his pony was dwarfed by the mighty warhorse, Perseus.

"I would speak with the master of this town!" he shouted at the helmeted guards above the grey stone gatehouse.

After some time, a silver-haired man in a red robe addressed him. "Sir, I am Cuneglasus of the Dobunni, chief magistrate of this town, appointed by Emperor Vortigern. State your business!"

Ambrosius removed his helmet and stared up at the old man. "Know this, Cuneglasus: that your master is dead, and I, Ambrosius Aurelius, High King of Britannia, am your lord and master. By my side is Prince Vortimer, the eldest of the deposed tyrant's sons. He will bear witness to the fate of his father and the fortress at Genoreu, destroyed by fire! Open your gates to us!"

Although a rider had informed him some hours earlier, the elderly man was still visibly distressed at the news, delivered in such harsh terms, and by his seemingly impossible position.

"My lord Ambrosius, this is disturbing news to my ears as the youth beside you is my nephew, and I grieve for the death of my brother. I am pleased that he has been spared the flames of Genoreu, but how many perished?"

Vortimer was prodded to speak. "My uncle, barely sixty escaped the flames, including my brother and sister, led to safety by Merlin and well received by our captor. We are in his hands now." His mournful voice tailed off, as silence befell them all.

"Then I must let you in, King Ambrosius, for I will not risk the same fate," Cuneglasus intoned.

TRIPHUN'S BOOMING LAUGH rang out and he slapped his new son-in-law firmly on the back. Ambrosius and his bride,

Gwendolyn, then danced in front of the assembled nobles of
Britannia in Kinarius's great hall in Caer Badon, the largest
complete stone building in the west. He had bowed to his
mother's dying wish and now had a queen. His alliance with the
powerful King Triphun was cemented, and he felt more secure
for it. No one publicly mourned the passing of Vortigern, or
questioned his rule.

Caer Badon proved a good location, where four Roman
roads met, and the town's taverns and guesthouses were filled
to overflowing. One month had passed since Vortigern's death
had been announced, and more tribal leaders from the north
and east had come to pay their homage to Ambrosius and asked
for his protection from raiders - not just the Saxons and Angles,
but also the Picts and Scotti from the north and west.

With all the leading nobles of the land in town, Ambrosius
had called a council meeting for the following day. This was his
first such meeting as high king, and was attended by twice as
many tribal leaders as the first such council meeting he had
attended in Calleva, where he introduced himself to Vortigern
as a Roman tribune, barely three years before. Much had
happened since then, and he now wore the purple robes and sat
on an elevated throne, looking down on his subjects who bowed
before speaking. It was clear from their submissions that fear of
invasion from Saxons, Jutes, Angles, Picts and the Scotti were
the main concerns.

In addition to familiar faces from the southern tribes,
Ambrosius was pleased to receive homage and pledges of
allegiance from the chiefs of the Coritani, Parisi and powerful
Brigantes tribes. Ambrosius had a whispered conversation with
Uther before addressing the council.

"My lords, I thank you for your pledges of loyalty, and for
the faith you place in me as your high king. I shall not use the
title 'Emperor', as I believe we must not look back to the days of

Rome, but forward as free men of Britannia. I vow to make safe my island kingdom, from both those who would invade us from without and those unwelcome hordes within."

Sporadic applause and some cheering broke out, but faces remained gravely set. Ambrosius was aware that some of the unhappy chiefs were from eastern lands already occupied by Angles and Saxons.

"To this end, I will lead my army north to swat away the bothersome Scotti and Pict invaders, and then make haste eastward to confront the Saxons, who are reported to advance up the east coast!"

This was what they wanted to hear, and all jumped to their feet, cheering, shouting and stamping on the paved stone floor.

After some time, he held up his hands for quiet. "I ask you all to provide warriors, both mounted and on foot, together with weapons and supplies. We shall rally on the plain outside of Corinium, twenty miles to the north of this place, in one month from now. Our northern allies may meet us at Deva or on the road to Eboracum. Go and prepare for war!"

ESTHER AND JESSICA had taken the young Queen Gwendolyn under their wing. They now represented the new royalty in the land and set about ordering new clothing and woven tapestries depicting the coat of arms of the queen. They adopted the lily as her symbol and created banners in light, bright colours that broke up the dominance of red, black and brown in the royal palace, where all about them were depictions of bears grappling with dragons.

Esther, leaving the queen's chamber, turned and unexpectedly bumped into her husband.

"Brian! You startled me! What are you doing? Why are you here?"

"My love, I was just passing and thought I would enquire about the queen's good health," he replied, stumbling over his words.

She narrowed her eyes and said, "You cannot fool me with your 'just passing'. What is it you wish to know of the queen?"

"Well, um, just to hear that our king and queen are, erm, happy together?" he stammered.

"Ah-ha!" she snorted, grabbing his arm and leading him to a quiet corner. "I know what you and Uther want to know. Shame on you both for thinking our brave King Ambrosius is not man enough to make an heir! Well, I can tell you he is!"

Brian looked about furtively and whispered, "My love, you know me too well and I cannot lie to you. You must keep this in confidence. I am concerned, as a brother, that our lord and king shall make of this a good match and finds his queen as pleasing in the bed chamber as I do you, my love." He beamed his self-satisfaction with his delicate choice of words.

Esther smothered a smirk and then scolded him. "Shame on you for ever doubting him. He is more than a man, and I can tell you that the queen is satisfied and hopes for a child. Go and tell that to Uther, but mind he keeps it from court gossip. Go!"

Brian marched from the new extended quarters across the large space that was once the Roman governor's hall in Corinium, now a royal palace with a new stone tower that afforded views over the countryside. The town was a busy, bustling centre of trade, with the newer Atrebates residents mingling seamlessly with their Dobunni tribal cousins. The plague had gone, and many saw it as a sign of good times under their king and queen. The young king of the Atrebates, Eliduris, one of the king's councilors, was placed in charge of the town, and of the safety of the queen and her attendants, over the town clerk, Morvidius. Ambrosius was pleased with the warm welcome afforded to his new wife and turned his attentions to preparing the army to take to the road.

Ambrosius, together with Uther, Brian and Dunstan, stood on the parapet of his castlleated tower and gazed out with satisfaction over the plain filled with tents and a thronging mass of soldiers and camp followers. More were still arriving.

"Uther, what is the latest number of fighting men in our ranks?"

Uther leaned forward on the wooden rail, bending it outwards with his powerful forearms.

"We have over ten thousand now, my brother," he boomed, "and as you can see, our ranks continue to swell."

A hawk circled above the plain, scattering a cloud of starlings. "It is a good omen," Brian said, looking up.

"My lord, may I speak?" Drustan asked. All eyes turned on the knight.

"Of course, noble Drustan, what thoughts are in your head?" Ambrosius said.

He coughed slightly and began, "With so many warriors at your disposal, and with regard to your desire to keep the borders of your kingdom secure, I wondered if you might give me leave to patrol our south coast whilst you ride north, my king?"

Ambrosius looked at him, his mind formulating a reply. "It is not such an unwelcome idea, Drustan, as I had expected to take an army of about eight thousand warriors to the northern borders. We get frequent reports of raids from the Jutes, who have made good their base in our Isle of Vectis. I might charge you with removing them once and for all. What say you?"

Drustan beamed his pleasure at the proposition. "My lord! It is a great and noble charge you give me, and I shall willingly undertake it. May I also be accompanied by Sir Percival, whose unit is made of stout men from the Regnii and Durotrigans? It is their lands we wish to defend, my lord."

"You ask for too much!" Uther roared, bringing his fist down on the wobbling rail.

Ambrosius raised a halting hand, "Dear Uther, be calmed."

Turning to Drustan he said, "You may go with Sir Percival, but do not take more than one thousand and five hundred men, all of whom must be mounted. But first you must ride east, on the Portway, to King Brennus, and check on his defences. Then ride south to King Elafius and brief him on our plans. From there continue south to our fortress at Portus Adurni. Secure the garrison and find or build enough ships for your invasion of the Isle of Vectis. These are your orders, Sir Drustan. Go and make your preparations."

Two days later, Sir Drustan and Sir Percival rode out to wild applause from the townsfolk and loitering warriors, their colourful pennants fluttering on the end of long lances. Ambrosius needed a few more days to give basic training to his new recruits, and blend them into existing units, under the watchful eyes of his busy knights. He was happy to pass the pressure of preparations onto his new unit commanders, and play them off against each other, to ensure they were well prepared both militarily and logistically.

Ambrosius and Uther were finally in agreement; they were ready. Ambrosius addressed the court before his departure.

"In my absence, my councillor, King Eliduris, will represent me, in consultation with my queen, Gwendolyn. Morvidius will continue to run the affairs of the town as clerk."

He paused to gaze over the receptive audience. "I have appointed the former innkeeper from Calleva, Brutus, as the new town clerk in Caer Gloui, or Glouvia as some call it. The offspring and most strident followers of Vortigern shall remain under guard, except for Vortimer, who will accompany me, as a second squire, under the supervision of my faithful Gawain."

Ambrosius sat on his throne to signal the end of the briefing, and the courtiers began to mingle with the knights.

Uther took Brian to one side and whispered, "Surely our noble brother has moved on from his youthful ways? He now has a wife and a responsibility to lead by example, according to his own code."

Brian tried to soothe him. "My brother, be calmed. He may enjoy the company of fine young men, but he has surely changed. Still, I feel we may have to watch over him and ensure there is no idle talk to undermine his leadership. Almost all the tribal chiefs of our land have rallied to his banner. We must be the guardians of his good name, for all our sakes."

Uther shrugged and said, "At least he has shown some good judgment in bringing the chief of Glouvia, Cuneglasus, and his family here under guard, and assimilating their warriors into our units."

"Indeed," Brian concurred, "and has chosen well with picking Brutus, our former innkeeper, who is a strong soldier and good organizer. He has sent him with a fresh detachment of loyal soldiers."

They joined the throng of knights saying farewell to family and friends, eager to ride out at the head of a large army in the morning.

"WE MUST HAVE every horse in your kingdom, my lord!" Tomos quipped, as the group of commanders watched their ranks of men, half mounted and half on foot, marching slowly off the plain. In truth, the Roman road running north-east, the Fosse Way, was only wide enough for two riders or four marching men abreast, followed by carts of supplies pulled by oxen, so progress would be slow.

"These roads were built for moving legions around this island, and we shall again put them to this use," Ambrosius said, smiling with pride at his army. "We have more men now than when we defeated Vortigern and his Saxons at Guloph. No one will stand in our way!"

They would march for two days before reaching the crossroads at Venonis, believed to be the centre of the island. From here, they would take Watling Street to the north-west, to the former Roman town of Deva, believed to be occupied by Scotti raiders from Hibernia.

At Venonis, a small settlement of traders had grown around the crossroads. Here they camped for two days, taking on more supplies. Ambrosius received the sons of the murdered kings, Jago and Gorbonuc, eager for the chance to avenge their fathers, and other disposed nobles from eastern lands. Also, King Brennus of the Catuvellauni rode in with his escort of four hundred mounted warriors.

"You are most welcome, King Brennus!" Ambrosius beamed, showing his pleasure at the arrival of the one-time ally of Vortigern.

"My lord, I have come to welcome you to the northern part of my lands, and to join you with my guard. And my thanks to you for sending your noble knights, Drustan and Percival, to check on our defences. They left satisfied, just this morning. Now I am at your service."

"This is a powerful ally," Uther muttered to Brian, "one who can raise the countryside to our cause."

Ambrosius was keen to talk to Brennus about what he knew of the lands they were marching towards.

"We are leaving my tribal lands here, at the crossroads, and entering the lands of King Virico of the Cornovii. My relationship with him has been difficult, to say the least, as they are thieves and raiders and a cause of much grief to my people. However, I will make an introduction to you of him, as he is very wary of all strangers to his lands, many of whom never return. You may recall, Virico was a staunch ally of Vortigern, present at the Battle of Guloph, where you killed or enslaved many of his finest warriors."

"I see," Ambrosius said, popping a dried piece of fruit into his mouth as they sat around the command table in his tent. "Do you think his warriors might attack us?"

"It is doubtful, my lord," Brennus replied. "They are not ones for open warfare, although you may find your supplies disappearing in the night."

Ambrosius unrolled his parchment map of Roman Britannia and pointed to the garrison town of Deva, at the end of Watling Street.

"And what do you know of the inhabitants of Deva?" he asked.

Brennus replied, "I have heard reports that seaborne raiders from Hibernia, the Scotti, now occupy that town. King Virico is based here, some thirty miles south of Deva. We can pass by it on our way by taking thios road." He pointed to a garrison town near the mountainous borders of Dyfed, called Viroconium.

Ambrosius turned to his men. "So it is settled. Tomorrow we break camp and go to this next town, Letocetum. From there it is another day's march to Viroconium, where this King Virico will surely be waiting for us."

"And then we shall discover the nature of our welcome," Brennus added.

Ambrosius dismissed his commanders and called for the sons of Jago and Gorbonuc, asking Brennus to stay. He asked them what they knew of the Saxon army.

"My lord, I am Alan, son of Jago." The confident young man with a mop of brown unkempt hair, bowed low. "We have tracked the army of Hengist moving north from Camulodunum. He has taken some four thousand men, most on foot. He has left a small garrison in the palace of Vortigern with Queen Rowena."

Ambrosius asked, "What else can you tell me?"

Another youth spoke up, "My king, our scouts tell us Hengist is gathering up as many of the Angle settlers as he can to swell his army."

"What do you know of these Angles?" Ambrosius probed.

Alan replied, "They are another Germanic tribe, neighbours of the Saxons, with grievances against them. They have settled along our east coast and look to push inland, looking for farming land. Some of our followers have been displaced from their homesteads by them and have come to fight."

"Good," Ambrosius said, "the more who rally to our cause, the better. We shall push these Angles and Saxons back into the Germanic Sea whence they came!"

11. Two Armies March

STARTLED BIRDS TOOK to the air, the last living things to flee before the ominous, steady drumbeat of the advancing Saxon army. A bitter wind blew across the desolate flat lands and low lying marshes of eastern Britannia as a straight, paved road guided the invaders to the former garrison town of Lindum. Hengist, sitting high on a powerful grey warhorse, called his sons, Octa and Eosa, and nephew, Ella, eager young men restless for action, to his side.

"You see, I told you we had no need for maps. The Romans linked all settlements by roads. Ride ahead with your men to see who is there. It could be locals or Angles. Either way, do not slay them. I would speak with their leader."

Hengist waved his arms, pointing to the cultivated plain before the gates of the walled town, indicating his men should spread out and wait.

Half an hour later, Octa rode out to speak to him; "Father, the town is occupied by an Angle chief called Wilfred. He invites you to join him as his guest."

"That was easy," Hengist growled. "Let's go."

They entered through a stone gatehouse, guarded by Angle warriors in quilted body armour and conical helmets, holding long spears. They crossed an open space to the steps of a stone building. Hengist dismounted and was greeted by a tall chief with twin braids on his long brown beard.

"You are welcome, Lord Hengist. Your reputation precedes you," he gushed, bowing to show his subservience to the powerful warlord. Hengist grunted and brushed past him into the dimly lit hall.

As his eyes adjusted to the gloom, Hengist walked towards the seat of power, a throne on an elevated wooden platform, and sat down. His sons and other commanders stood before him, and Wilfred hovered uncomfortably at his side.

"Bring mead and ale! My men are thirsty!" Hengist bellowed, as his men roared their approval. They drank and ate what was brought from the kitchen, and after a while the Saxon chief beckoned Wilfred to come close.

"How many warriors do you have, Wilfred the Angle?"

Wilfred knew where this line of questioning was going. "My lord, I come from a small village in Angeln, and have but fifty followers to my name. We came some two years ago and marched inland from a river estuary to find this town unguarded, with but a few locals living a frugal existence."

Hengist glared at him. "So you now have a town, taken without a fight. Do you make the locals work and farm for you?"

"My lord," he replied, "there was no chief here, merely a frightened headman, who accepted my offer of protection and meekly submitted to my rule. They work their fields and we have revived the forge with our blacksmith, and all must pay a tithe to my hall."

The hulking Saxon cleared his throat in a phlegmy cough, spat on a yelping dog and shifted awkwardly in his bearskin cloak. "So you have an easy life, living off the backs of these trembling sheep. That is good. We shall soon rule over this land, and our common ties and belief in Woden and Valhalla will bind us into one. We shall enjoy your hospitality, Wilfred, for two days, then continue our march north. I have heard there is a city along this road?"

"There is my lord," he readily assured the Saxon, "a large walled town the Romans called Eboracum. Some two days' march onwards. Whoever holds that place commands the north of this island."

"Then we shall proceed there," Hengist said, draining his mug of mead and wiping the froth off his gritty beard with the back of his hand.

"It is my great pleasure to host you and your men, my lord," Wilfred gushed, relieved at the shortness of the stay. "My servants will send food and drink to your soldiers without."

"Water only for them," Hengist said, grabbing Wilfred's sleeve, "I don't want them drunk. Not until they have blood on their swords and axes. Oh, and I shall take your best fighting men with me." He grinned at his host, who scurried away to make the arrangements.

ANIMAL SKULLS AND dead crows hung from lifeless trees and an eerie silence greeted Ambrosius and his army as they approached the fortress at Viroconium. In the foothills of the wild mountains of Dyfed, it was an imposing presence on an otherwise bleak and deserted landscape.

Calling forward Tomos, Ambrosius said, "Send riders ahead to announce our presence."

Ambrosius noticed the soft, boggy ground on either side of the track that lead to the gate of the fortress. It provided a natural defence. As Tomos and a dozen riders approached the bleak stone walls, they were met with a hail of arrows. Most were able to raise their shields in time to take the impact. A horse whinnied in pain and reared up as an arrow pierced its neck, unseating its rider. Another soldier cried out as an arrow lodged in his thigh.

Tomos helped his fallen man onto his horse as they turned and fled out of arrow range. The wounded horse bucked and neighed as it bolted into the soggy marsh, sinking up to its knees, stuck and twisting in its agony. The archers proceeded to use the unfortunate animal for target practice, peppering its body with arrows until it folded to the ground.

"This is a hostile welcome," Uther growled. Ambrosius nodded his agreement, and summoned the returned Tomos to him.

"What can you tell me of this devilish fortress?" he asked.

Tomos replied, "My lord, a score of archers lay in wait and fired directly at us as we approached. I saw no commander and heard no orders shouted. My man is wounded but will live."

"This is indeed a rude welcome. Let us retire to firm ground and discuss our options. Where is my engineer, Sir Brastius?"

A short stout knight rode to him, gathering all the dignity he could muster, a long drooping moustache dangling from his earnest face beneath a Roman helmet. In that instant, Ambrosius knew he had to design a new, standard helmet for his randomly attired followers. Each knight had a motif on their standard, and his was the boar.

Ambrosius addressed him. "Brastius, take your men and survey the outside of this fortress, noting all details of it, areas of weakness and your best estimate of numbers within."

The knight bowed and withdrew, and Ambrosius went about posting guards on the approach to the fortress before leading his men to a field behind a screen of trees.

Calling his commanders to him, he said, "What advice can you give me?" They all dismounted and stood in a circle: Uther, Brian and the assembled knights who had not been given tasks.

Uther was quick to answer. "My brother, we should fire burning missiles over their walls and set their buildings alight! It worked last time."

Brian was more considered. "Certainly, an assault on this imposing fortress, built on a rocky outcrop above marshy land, would be difficult. He looked Ambrosius in the eye. "It could be costly in the lives of our men."

Ambrosius looked along the line of tight-lipped knights until Sir Owain spoke. "My lord, this is an act of defiance in your kingdom, and this Chief Virico, who is known to us," glancing at Cadeyrn, "has raided our borders and made off with our livestock and womenfolk, causing much distress."

Cadeyrn added, "Aye, my lord, we would welcome the chance to free our people and bring this villain low."

"If we could somehow get inside..." Brian pondered.

"Perhaps there is a way," said a voice from outside the group. They all looked in the direction from where it came and were astounded to see the healer taken prisoner at Genoreu.

"Merlin, what are you doing here?" Ambrosius asked, incredulous.

"Do not be angry with me, my lord, for I came to offer my assistance to you in your quest to unify your kingdom. I have knowledge of these lands, for I have travelled far, and my counsel may be of use to you."

"Impertinent wretch!" Uther stormed. "You have disobeyed the king's command to remain in Corinium! How dare you leave without consent and present yourself in a bold and insolent manner. You will be flayed for this!"

"Hold, my brother," Ambrosius said, "let us first hear his idea for gaining entry. Speak, Merlin."

The tall, thin man pushed back the sleeves of his grey cowl and dropped the hood to reveal his shock of unkempt brown hair. "My lord, I have been inside this fortress, and know there is a rear entrance through a tunnel hewn from the rocks. I can lead a small force of your men there, then through the town to the main gate where we shall open it."

"You make it sound so simple," Brian said. "How will a group of soldiers move across the town undetected, even assuming you can gain entrance through what must be a locked doorway?"

"Can we trust him, my lord?" Sir Bagdemagus said. "He was Vortigern's loyal aide until recently."

Ambrosius put the question to Merlin. "Well? Why should we trust you, Merlin?"

All stared at the curious man, taking in his thin, bony features and piercing grey eyes, wondering how old he was and where had he come from to look so unusual.

Merlin focussed his steady gaze on Ambrosius, something few had the nerve to do. "My noble lord, I am your servant and follower. For long, it has been foretold that a strong and wise king would arise to unite the people against a foreign foe. I have known for many years that Vortigern was not that king. You are that king, and I am at your service." He bowed low and stood in silence.

"Sorcerer!" Uther yelled. "You are a shaman from the forests of Dyfed, behind these mountains, a druid who worships the trees and stars. You have loyalty to no one!"

Ambrosius raised a hand and spoke. "My brother is right, Merlin. You appear out of nowhere, in defiance of my orders, and expect me to trust you in this plan. Furthermore, I know not under what circumstances you came to be in Vortigern's service. You could betray my men to the enemy. I would be a fool to trust you. Guards! Seize him!"

Four guards grabbed him and led him away. Ambrosius turned back to his group and proposed they make camp for the night and further discuss the matter over their evening meal. Merlin's unexpected appearance and forthright manner of speech disturbed him, and was still in his mind when, an hour later, Tomos found him resting in his tent.

"My lord, may I speak?" he said.

"Of course, Tomos, come in."

"This strange man, whether wizard or healer, may be sincere in his protestation. The only way to find out is for someone to go with him to establish if this tunnel exists and if it leads to a doorway or gate. Otherwise, you could have him whipped or strangled, and then we would never know. I volunteer to go with him, in the dark of night, to survey the rear of the fortress and assess the situation."

Ambrosius looked at his wiry, scar-faced aide with admiration. "You are a fine and loyal soldier, Tomos, and I always trust your judgement. There is something about this Merlin that intrigues me. He speaks few words, but they are always well-chosen and have a ring of wisdom about them. This would be a dangerous assignment and I would not wish to lose you this way..."

His voice trailed away and Tomos spoke, "My lord, I am first and foremost a soldier, skilled in the ways of the Roman legions, and with an instinct for survival. I feel I can handle this matter, and should it be a trap, I shall kill the wretch and hide in the mountains. I cannot see any other way, except to gain secret entry to the place and open the gates."

Ambrosius reflected in silence for a moment. "Aye, an assault would be difficult, but not impossible. I would send someone else on this mission, but I know you are the one with the skills and instincts to survive it. Perhaps a team of three men? Who else would you take?"

Tomos smiled, showing a gap in his front teeth. "My lord, I would take our gladiator, Ursus, to keep an eye on the prisoner, and an engineer, such as Sir Brastius, to survey the walls of the tunnel."

"By the gods!" Ambrosius exclaimed. "Must I lose three good men in this venture?"

"When we roll the dice, we expect to win," Tomos replied.

"It is the way of the legions," Ambrosius said, nodding his assent. "Then you must go tonight, but first, bring this Merlin to me so we may question him some more."

When Merlin was just as persuasive a second time, it was agreed that this would be a reconnaissance mission only, with positively no engagement with the enemy, nor risk of discovery. They must dress in black and blacken their faces, carry only daggers, and be prepared for a quick escape. Uther was doubtful, but conceded it was worth a try.

WORD OF THE approaching Saxon army spread like a warning of plague as they marched steadily north, passing nothing but deserted farmsteads. They took what they could find, piling wooden doors and beams onto oxcarts, and kept on marching, finally arriving at the fortified town of Eboracum. The wooden gates were barred and the battlements manned by stern-faced warriors.

"At last," Hengist said with a smile to his sons, "someone to fight." He gave his instructions for the army to set up camp before the main gate, and told Ella to take some men and ride around the fortress, noting its features.

An hour later, Ella returned. "My chief, the fortress is, as seen, made of a high earth bank with sharpened wooden stakes all around forming a stockade. The two walls to the side are narrower in length than this one before us. There is an open dry ditch all around, save for a stream that runs through, and four gates, one on each side."

"You have a good eye for detail, young Ella," Hengist noted. "And did you notice any areas of weakness?"

Ella considered this before replying. "I think those within must defend all four gates, and also the opening where the stream cuts through the bank. Only a handful of warriors could enter through the stream and would be cut down..."

Hengist stopped him there. "You have given us the key to this. They have six points of entry, which they must defend, and we shall attack them at all six points to test their strength. Now, let the men eat roasted meat for tomorrow we attack this fortress!"

TOMOS LED HIS small band by the light of a hazy half-moon, along a track running south from their camp. The snuffles of forest animals, the hooting of owls and the steady crunch of twigs under the hooves of their mounts were the sounds that accompanied them as they turned west towards the fortress. Merlin suggested following the tree line to the south of the fortress, before crossing a stream and climbing into the foothills behind the imposing dark shape, ever to their right.

Merlin had picked out a track that guided them around rocks as they rode to a position high up behind the fortress.

"Let us dismount here, Sir Tomos," he whispered. Sporadically, the darkness was relieved when a shaft of moonlight escaped through the clouds, enough for them to find their way into a gulley with a sparse covering of grass and some small withered trees, to which they tethered the horses.

"This way," Merlin said, making to walk away.

Tomos grabbed his sleeve. "Not so fast, Merlin; I'll do the leading."

They scrambled down scree slopes, getting ever closer to the rear wall of the fortress. Twin towers on the corners were silhouetted against the night sky when the intermittent pale moon shone.

"Soon the moon will leave us, giving two hours of blackness before dawn. We must hurry," Merlin whispered in his harsh Brythonic tongue. He pointed the way and Tomos stumbled on, trying his best to avoid kicking stones downhill. After ten minutes Merlin tapped him on the shoulder.

"It is near. Somewhere here I think..." He stood straight and moved his head around, as if having the ability to see in the dark. The other three watched him warily. "Over there," he said, pointing to a dark gulley.

They entered the gulley in pitch darkness, each having to brush the sharp, rocky wall with their hand. Tomos walked blindly, trusting to Mithras to guide him. A sudden shaft of moonlight made him stop in his tracks. Before him was a metal grid stretching across the gulley, with a wooden door in the centre. He waited until they were all together. A whispered discussion took place between the four.

"We have completed our mission," Brastius hissed. "Let us withdraw."

"But we know not where this leads," Tomos said, peering into the darkness beyond the grid.

"I can open the door if you wish?" Merlin offered.

"It is a trick!" the hulking Ursus muttered.

"Quiet!" Tomos hissed. "You say you can open this door, Merlin; then do it."

Merlin pulled something from a hidden pocket in his cowl and set to work on the large keyhole in the door. The others stood around him, listening for sounds other than the occasional click of the lock. After barely thirty seconds, a final click saw Merlin push the door slightly ajar.

"Let me go first," Tomos said, edging past him.

The rusted hinges creaked as he made enough of a gap to slip into the darkness beyond. Brastius followed, then Merlin and Ursus. The passageway was man-made with smooth finishes to the walls and a paved path. Cobwebs brushed Tomos's face, a sign that the tunnel had not been used for some time. They crept forward slowly, following the tunnel downwards. Tomos counted fifty steps before they came to what appeared to be the rear wall of the fortress. There was another similar wooden door in the stone wall. He whispered to Brastius who placed both palms on the walls and moved sideways, as if examining it.

Tomos spoke quietly to Merlin who again tried his trick on the lock.

"It will not open," he whispered. "There is a key in the lock on the other side, turned so I cannot push it out."

Tomos realised there was little else they could do, so he indicated they should withdraw. They retraced their steps without incident and found their horses, leading them down the mountainside and riding away before the first signs of dawn marked their return to camp.

Tomos led the group to a campfire that they shared with a shivering guard. They would wait until Ambrosius awoke and emerged from his tent, drinking hot soup with chunks of bread, content that their mission had been a success and Merlin had proved himself a reliable ally.

IT TOOK HENGIST barely half a day to gain entry to the fortified town, gamely defended by two thousand Brigante warriors led by a brave chief. That chief's head was now impaled on a stake above the main gates, along with his commanders.

The Saxon army had forced its way through an opening made for a stream at the far side of the fortress, and barged their way through one of the side gates, using roof beams as battering rams and doors as shields for their warriors to deflect arrows and spears. Once inside, a desperate defence was crushed by brutal sword and axe blows, and the other gates opened. Men were slaughtered, women raped and children corralled into pens to be used, or sold, as slaves.

Hengist gave strict orders that the town should not be set alight, as they would look to hold it as their northern base. Several nights of feasting and drinking for his men had been earned.

After three days of drunken revelry, when the cries of the slowly tortured captives had died out, a scout arrived with news. Hengist roused himself and asked that a pail of water be poured over his head to stimulate his senses before he let the rider speak.

"My lord, there is a large army approaching from the south and west," the scout blurted out.

Hengist shook the water from his greasy hair, his blond braids swinging in the gloomy light of the hall.

"When you say 'large army', how many men are you talking of?" he growled.

"I saw more men than you have, my lord," was the hurried reply.

"Hmmm, an army of more than five thousand men. That could only be Ambrosius, the king who bettered the feeble Vortigern in battle, killing many of our own. Let us hope it is him, and his brother Uther, slayer of my brother, Horsa. I would have both their heads mounted on my gatepost!"

Eosa appeared at his side and asked, "Father, shall we prepare to defend the town?"

"No, my son," he replied. "We shall not be trapped like cornered rats in this place. We shall take to the field and meet them in open battle, as is our way.

Tell the men to sober up; we leave in the morning!"

12. Maisbeli

TWO WEEKS HAD passed since Ambrosius had recorded a decisive victory over the rebel chief Virico and had found the town of Deva deserted. Scotti raiders had retreated at news of their approach. Uther had taken great delight in riding down some of the fleeing Hibernians as they ran to their boats. Brian and his archers had joined in the slaughter, also managing to set fire to some of their boats with burning arrows as they attempted to escape on a narrow river that led to the northern sea.

"They shall not return soon," Brian had remarked, just as two boats eluded them, rowing hard and then setting their sails as they entered a wide estuary.

Ambrosius's army of eight thousand was now moving across the island, heading east on a well-kept road. He called Tomos to his side.

"We shall soon be at Eboracum, a city I have heard much about from Marcus. His father fought there with the ninth legion, who built a mighty wall defining the northern border of the Roman Empire. The Brigantes who inhabit these parts are a wild and lawless tribe, and the Picts beyond the wall are even wilder. We are truly approaching the ends of the world."

He patted his horse and smiled at his most loyal deputy. "I have been meaning to congratulate you, Sir Tomos," he said, "for expertly leading your men through the tunnel at Virocorum and fighting your way to the main gate to let us in. Thankfully, their soldiers quickly gave up and willingly surrendered their unpopular chief to us."

"Ha ha!" Tomos chortled, "He did not command the respect of his followers as you do, my lord. It was a swift battle. Now his unsmiling head stands on their gate as a warning to those who oppose your rule."

"And many captives were released," Ambrosius added. "Cadeyrn was pleased to provide a new garrison of his men for the fort." He smiled as he patted the downy neck of Perseus.

Their paved road took them to the south of a range of mountains, past clusters of dour-faced peasants who gawped in awe at the mixed Romano-Briton army as it passed. Embroidered banners on wooden poles had replaced the golden eagles of the legions, and cavalry units sported different coloured pennants on their lances.

"Our biggest test lies ahead of us, when we meet the Saxons in battle," Ambrosius remarked. "They shall not run from us like those pox-ridden raiders."

Three scouts came in a hurry, halting their wide-eyed and foam-mouthed horses in front of Ambrosius and Tomos. Uther and Brian quickly joined them. A group of thirty or more armed warriors, wearing wolf and bearskins over their armour, followed them at a short distance.

"My lord, the Saxon army is ahead!" a young man panted, gagging on dust.

"To arms!" Uther shouted, "You are being followed!"

"My lord, do not attack them!" pleaded the scout, "They are Brigantes warriors who have fled Eboracum. That town is now in Saxon hands," he puffed.

"How far are the Saxons?" Ambrosius demanded.

"They are barely eight miles hence, and number at least five thousand."

"Then we must find a field in which to meet them," Ambrosius said. "Brian, lead your men out to look for flat land, perhaps with a hill to one side. Go swiftly!"

The order to halt had been passed down the line, and Ambrosius now awaited the report from the Brigantes. They pulled up on tired horses and their leader spoke.

"My king, I am Isurium, a son of King Getterix of the Brigantes. I bring news that the Saxon army has taken Eboracum and there has been great slaughter of my people. There is no news of my father and older brothers, but I fear few were spared. There is no Brigante army to fight under your banner, my lord, except we few who were on patrol when we saw the smoke from our burning town."

Uther growled his anger at the young man's sorrowful report. "This makes our task harder without the men of the north," he muttered.

"We shall manage," Ambrosius replied. "Tell the men to prepare to leave the road. There may be rough terrain but my guess is our way lies to the south, where the land is less mountainous. Let us rest awhile and await Brian's report. Isurium, your men shall join us. Seek refreshment at the rear."

After some thirty minutes, Brian returned and advised of a suitable location.

"My lord, there is a wide plain, with a stream running through, used for cattle grazing by some locals. I asked them the name of the place, and they replied, 'Maisbeli'."

"I hope you urged them to remove their cattle and flee," Uther said.

"Indeed I did, brother Uther. I will lead you there."

The army turned off the road onto a dusty track in single file. They were grateful for the dry earth beneath their feet, and the ox carts were able to manage the way between stands of trees and past thatched houses and farmsteads. Children ran beside the soldiers, laughing and whooping with delight as the sun shone down on the purposeful army.

"We shall make our command position on that hillock," Ambrosius said, pointing to his right. "Our foot soldiers should occupy the foreground facing the stream. If we can goad them to attack us, then they must ford that stream. Brian and Owain, position your archers behind our foot soldiers but within range of the stream. That is where we shall fire on them."

Uther eyed the flat meadow with a grin and said, "This is good ground for our horses. Shall we keep some of our riders in reserve, my brother?"

"You know me too well, Uther," Ambrosius remarked. "Yes, perhaps half should remain hidden behind the screen of trees to our back, to be deployed at a decisive moment in the battle. You may organise this. I will set up the command post. Tomos, I want your unit in the centre of our shield wall, to take the main thrust of our enemy's ire."

When all his knights stood before him, Ambrosius issued them with their orders. "We have ten units, four of cavalry and six of foot. Uther will be overall commander of the four cavalry units and shall deploy them, some in view of our enemy, and some in reserve. I shall command the foot soldiers."

He surveyed the keen faces before him and continued, "Our shield wall shall be under the command of Sir Tomos and shall, in addition to his own unit, comprise the units of Bagdemagus, Brastius, Bors and Pelleas. They shall take the brunt of the Saxon shield wall, as we expect them to take us head on in a show of force."

Smirks of anticipation were exchanged by the grizzled legion veterans.

Ambrosius regarded his commanders with pride for a moment, but quickly reverted to business.

"The cavalry units of Brian, Owain, Cadeyrn and Tristan will report to Uther. That leaves Kay whose unit will form my personal guard and act as reserve. The only other matter is how we draw the Saxon army onto yonder field." He nodded towards the stream and screen of bushes that divided the open space in two. In the distance, cattle herders were driving their animals away.

Uther made a suggestion. "My lord brother, we could lead them here with our mounted archers harassing them. The Saxons will chase anyone who opposes them!" The knights shared a laugh at this.

Ambrosius said, "You are right, Uther, they will send riders after our riders, but will Hengist follow them blindly with his army?"

"They will be looking for a fight, my lord," Brian offered. "That is their way."

"Perhaps it is that simple," Ambrosius mused, his gaze lifting above their heads to the clear blue sky. "And it is perfect conditions for a fight! Let us make ready!"

The men cheered their king and noisily dispersed.

BRIAN STARED HARD at the trail of marching warriors, led by a dozen drummers, emerging from a cloud of dust.

"They want all to know they are coming," he dryly observed to Cadeyrn.

"Saxons fear no one and think they will always win a fight. That is our advantage," Cadeyrn observed. "Let us prepare our archers to attack."

The Saxon army was also marching along the Roman road from Eboracum, heading west. Now Brian and Cadeyrn had to divert them some ten miles to the south, towards the meadow at Maisbeli.

"My lords, Saxons!" came a cry from a rider hurrying towards them along the Ridgeway on which they were positioned. Brian and Drustan reined back their horses to see some of their men fleeing before a band of determined Saxons, some fifty paces away, who waved their lances and swords as they bore down on them.

"Let us flee before them and stop to engage them on yonder hill fort!" Brian shouted, spurring his horse into action.

A group of their men had been positioned there, some two miles distant. They galloped, gathering up their archers as they went. The ancient pathway guided them along the ridgeline to a crude wooden stockade.

"Form a line and prepare to fire!" Brian ordered, hurriedly dismounting in the stockade. The archers followed Cadeyrn, sweating under their leather caps and clutching their braced bows.

Predictably, the Saxons did not slow or hesitate, but charged straight at the archers, who fired volleys of arrows as they passed the one hundred paces mark.

"Lancers, prepare to step forward!" Brian yelled, as the surviving horsemen thundered towards them. A hastily convened rear rank of soldiers wielding long lances stepped forward as the archers ran to their horses.

"Cadeyrn, lead our mounted soldiers, I shall fight here on foot!" he yelled at his fellow commander.

With a roar of oaths and a clash of terrified horses, some impaled on lances, the two sides met. Hand-to-hand fighting broke out as unseated Saxons engaged with Brian and his men. Axes rained down on the Briton swordsmen who defended themselves with both skill and valour. Cadeyrn drove his men to attack the mounted Saxons from the side and rear, cutting them down. The small group of barely one hundred ungainly Saxon horsemen was soon overcome.

There was no time for celebrations as a thin trail of dust indicated more horsemen were approaching.

"Quickly, to horse!" Brian shouted, helping a wounded soldier to mount. "Let us retreat!"

At Maisbeli field, Ambrosius sat silently on Perseus, flanked by Uther, Tomos and Kay, their preparations made and their troops laid out before them in ranks, ready to fight.

"Riders approach!" yelled a scout, as rising dust in the distance drew everyone's eyes.

"Hold your fire! Our riders are coming!" Ambrosius yelled, and the order was echoed along the lines of eager archers.

Brian and Cadeyrn had reached the stream and managed to negotiate the fall and rise, although some riders rushed too fast and were thrown.

A horn blast from the Saxon army checked the charge of their horsemen, who halted before the stream, allowing the fallen Britons to escape, as they surveyed the Briton army before them.

There was an eerie quiet, devoid of nature, disturbed now by the steady drumbeat of the marching Saxon army who filed onto the far meadow. They arranged themselves into clusters, each group under a mounted thane. Amidst much shouting, the foot soldiers lined up behind large oval shields in ranks three deep, their metal bosses and helmets glinting in the sunlight.

"We will mock them. Tell your men to drum a beat on their shields," Ambrosius instructed Tomos.

Soon there were steady pounded rhythms on both sides of the divided meadow. Pennants and banners fluttered limply in the weak breeze. Buzzards circled high into the blue above, in anticipation.

"They are grouped by the village they hail from, my lord," Kay observed, pointing out the different coloured banners in each unit.

"I care not where they hail from," Uther growled, "only that it is a good day to fight and kill Saxons."

Horn blasts announced the advance of the Saxon front line, braying in time with the drumbeats. Ambrosius and Tomos quickly agreed the line was two hundred men wide, with an unknown number of ranks behind. Their mounted soldiers were lined up behind. Tomos rode off to speak with his fellow commanders and prepare to meet the determined advance.

Ambrosius turned to his brother. "Uther, ready your cavalry, but they must not throw their javelins until the front rank of the enemy is in the stream. May God be with you." The two men clasped forearms and Uther rode away. "Owain, your archers must fire on their front ranks when they are in the stream."

Turning to Brian and Cadeyrn, who had arrived at the command post on the hillock, Ambrosius welcomed them.

"Well met, dear brother Brian and noble Cadeyrn – I see your mission was a success! We have drawn the bear to the hive; now we must sting it. Hide yourselves with the other riders, behind the trees, together with our Brigante allies, and wait for my signal to join the fray."

They bowed and departed, leaving Ambrosius and Kay to survey the field before them.

"We must inflict a heavy slaughter on them today, Sir Kay, if we are to free our island of this curse."

"Aye, my lord," was all Kay could think of in reply. His heart was pumping, his stomach clenched in a knot and his senses sharpened with anticipation of the fight. Their horses stamped and snorted, also primed and ready.

The Saxon front rank had passed the row of scrub and dropped into the stream, only their helmets showing to the waiting Britons. Owain gave the order and a hail of arrows were loosed, arching high over Tomos and his soldiers, raining death down on those struggling to get out of the stream. Ambrosius noticed movement to his far left. Enemy cavalry were fording the stream where it was narrowest, but Uther had already arranging his cavalry into two ranks, ready to meet them. On his order they trotted forward and threw their light javelins at the horsemen emerging from the stream. Amidst cries and screams, they galloped to meet their foe, swinging swords and maces.

Saxon foot soldiers clambered over the bodies of their dead comrades and formed a line with shields up, facing Tomos's shield wall. Arrows continued to rain down on those Saxons struggling to cross the deadly mire, but they were wiser now and held their shields over their heads. With a roar of angry defiance their commanders urged them to advance, until the two shield walls clashed in a deafening crash of metal bosses and wooden frames, mixed with the war cries of both armies.

Ambrosius looked on grimly, as the two walls pushed and shoved against each other, more men joining the rear ranks of both sides to lend their weight. It was to be a war of attrition. The rectangular roman shields of the Britons pressed firmly against the oval Saxon shields, and the front ranks sought opportunities to stab and slash at their foes.

The battle was well underway as both cavalry charges had clattered into each other, with fierce oaths and clashing of swords on shields, in what was now a melee of mounted warriors hacking at each other.

"Shall we send in the reserves?" Kay anxiously asked Ambrosius.

"Not yet, Sir Kay. We must draw them all onto the field of battle first."

Just then, a cry went up from their right flank. "Enemy riders approach!"

Ambrosius wheeled Perseus to his right at the sight of a large number of Saxon horsemen galloping straight towards them.

"Turn and face!" he yelled, as they had barely seconds to prepare. "You! Fetch Cadeyrn to our aid! Tell Brian to support Uther! Those are my orders!"

The thunder of hooves was all the warning they needed, and with a blood-curdling cry the Saxons were upon them. Ambrosius was surrounded by his loyal guard who fought off any attempts to reach him. He stood up in his stirrups looking for one who might be Hengist. Kay valiantly led his unit into the thick of it, flaying about him with his broadsword as Saxons attempted to smash through the raised shields of his men with their huge battle-axes.

With Excalibur raised, glinting in the sunlight, he spurred Perseus towards a well-built Saxon commander in a black bearskin cloak. He was savagely smashing through the neck guard of an unfortunate Briton. Seeming to sense the approach of Ambrosius, he freed his axe and swung around to face his charge. Excalibur came down on the thick haft, slicing half through it and causing the heavy blood-stained axe head to snap off.

Hengist growled and drew his sword in time to parry Ambrosius's next pass. They faced off and duelled with sword and shield, as a mad cacophony of violence reverberated around them. Ambrosius was lean but strong in arm, and able to match the giant Saxon blow for blow. Whilst still mounted on his fearless stallion, Ambrosius felt he had the advantage. He urged Perseus forward, ramming his breast plate into the flank of Hengist's grey mare, who threw back her head in pain, whinnying and staggering to her left, throwing her rider.

Ambrosius checked for cover, spying two of his guards, before heaving himself from his horse. He moved towards the big Saxon fumbling for his sword in the slick mud. The grey ran off, but Perseus stood close by, snorting and stamping.

Ambrosius brought Excalibur crashing down on Hengist's sword, but he took the blow and stood up. Roaring, he stumbled forwards in defiance. Seeing his plight, his sons jumped from their horses and they approached Ambrosius from two sides.

Ambrosius's loyal guards, two of the original Amorican soldiers with whom he had landed, countered this move. The adversaries slashed and grappled with each other, churning to mud the grassy meadow beneath their feet. Just then, Cadeyrn joined the fight, pushing his way past duelling warriors to reach Ambrosius and jump down by his side. Hengist laughed, as if this was the happiest moment of his life, and swung his sword at Ambrosius whilst punching his shield at Cadeyrn.

The Britons had overpowered the ill-equipped and unpracticed Saxon cavalry unit with superior skill and numerical advantage, and some riders now looked on as the two leaders slugged it out in the mud, surrounded by a ring of sword-wielding Briton soldiers. Soon, the only two still exchanging blows were Hengist and Ambrosius.

"Throw down your sword, Hengist, and submit!" Ambrosius shouted above the din.

Hengist groaned and strained behind a slow-motion slash, easily parried by the fitter Ambrosius.

"Your son is held by my men. See for yourself. I will spare him if you submit," he said, locking eyes with the seething Saxon chief. Hengist looked around him, seeing only a wall of Briton soldiers and dozens of his men disarmed and on their knees.

"If this is not my day, upstart king, then I would have you send me to Valhalla," he growled through gritted teeth.

"Then I will kill you, Hengist, but know this; I will give your sons the choice to leave my lands so your name will live on."

"I accept your terms, and would have you kill me with my sword in my hand!" With that, he roared one last time and ran at Ambrosius, bringing his sword down in a high swinging arc.

It was the move of a man knowing he was about to be killed, as Ambrosius easily side-stepped him and drove Excalibur through his leather jerkin and between his ribs. Hengist groaned and fell to his knees, his conical helmet falling before him and his greasy flaxen hair screening his face. The last sound he heard was Eosa's cry of 'Father!', as Ambrosius cleaved his head from his body.

Beyond the defeat of the Saxon cavalry, the battle still raged. As Ambrosius raised his head to look about him, he could hear the distant sounds of men fighting and dying.

"Hengist is dead, but the battle is not yet over!" he cried. "To arms!"

His men yelled a salute and turned to find their horses. Cadeyrn took charge of the situation and delegated a group of men to bind the prisoners and take them to the command post, along with the remains of Hengist.

Ambrosius mounted Perseus and rallied his escort. "Onwards to help our brothers!" he yelled, the blood pumping through his veins, his eyes wide on his blood-splattered face, eager for more action.

The victory was by no means certain and he was anxious for news of both Tomos and Uther, as two separate battles raged on the muddy meadow. He skirted the back of the shield wall tussle, as wounded men and those attending them dodged his black stallion. He saw one of Tomos's deputy commanders clutching his bleeding right arm against his chest.

"Hail fellow! What news of Tomos and the other knights?"

"My lord, they are all at the front, fighting for their lives against our enemy. The Saxons are strong and have no fear, but we are bettering them bit by bit. Sir Tomos was alive and giving orders when I was cut on my sword arm, my lord."

"Go and receive treatment at our command post, brave soldier!" he replied.

Ambrosius was already moving on, standing up in his stirrups to see over the heads of his soldiers. The shield wall had broken in some places and soldiers were fighting hand-to-hand, wielding swords, lances, daggers and axes. Many of the soldiers sliding into the mud would never scramble upright. A look of decision lit the king's eyes and, turning Perseus, he galloped to his command post.

Cadeyrn was there, organising a collection pen for prisoners.

"Bring me the head of Hengist!" Ambrosius shouted.

Two of Cadeyrn's men went scurrying and soon returned. One carried by its flaxen hair the head of Hengist, trailing its plaited beard in the dirt. The eyes were closed and the skin already turning grey. Ambrosius ordered Cadeyrn to rally as many mounted warriors as possible.

"We shall ride into the midst of the battle with Hengist's head raised on a lance," he shouted, "and cause the enemy to realise the day is ours and to throw down their weapons."

Cadeyrn responded, "My lord, perhaps some Saxon captives can be persuaded to spread the word in their own language, convince them their chief is dead and his sons captured." The nodding head of his leader encouraged him to add more. "Also, we can fix a cross-pole to the lance, beneath his head, and hang his bearskin cloak on the beam. They will see it truly is their chief."

"Yes, good idea, Cadeyrn. See to it!" Ambrosius was anxious to see out the day and claim victory without sacrificing more of his men in the bloody slaughter. "I shall ride to Uther and Brian."

He left Cadeyrn to his grisly task, took his escort of thirty guards, and rode to the far side of the wide meadow where the two cavalry armies had clashed. Wounded and dying men and horses littered the field through which they picked their way to where the fighting was thickest. Sure enough, Uther and Brian were fighting on foot, back to back, slashing and chopping at their opponents. The numbers still fighting were barely a hundred on each side, as many had perished or were badly wounded.

Ambrosius barged past staggering Saxons, occasionally chopping down on their heads with Excalibur, until he reached his two brothers. He indicated to his guard to engage with the enemy surrounding the two, clearing the way for him to jump down from Perseus and embrace them both.

"Hail brothers! We are winning the day! Hengist is dead and his sons captured, and Cadeyrn will soon display his head in the heart of the throng yonder." He indicated with his head the battle on foot by the muddy stream.

Uther's blood-splattered face was fixed in a grin, "My noble brother! This is fine work for soldiers, knights and kings!"

"Your coming is timely, my brother," panted the more prudent Brian. "We have been fighting for hours here with no news of how the battle was going. The Saxons are determined foe and have slain many of our finest men."

"They have come on us in great number and with grim resolve," Ambrosius said, looking cautiously about him. "We must end this slaughter before nightfall by winning the day. Let us mop up this group and join the main fight."

The brothers resumed fighting with vigour, after their brief rest, and before long the added impetus of the skilful royal guards had forced the exhausted Saxons to throw down their weapons. Leaving his deputies to round up prisoners, he led those still with fight in them to the killing ground.

The scene that greeted them was one of a massacre, with men's bodies and severed limbs littering the ground, and the groans of the dying filling their ears. After two hours of constant strife, few blows were being exchanged, and there was little shouting anymore. Broken shields and hafts littered the heart of the battlefield, and bodies were half-submerged in mud where they had been trampled on. The three brothers cut down many Saxons as they advanced in a line with their determined men, until they came upon a stand-off between two sets of blood-soaked and muddy warriors. Cadeyrn and a handful of riders were displaying the grizzly head of Hengist on a pole with his cloak hanging limply below. The ghostly image of the powerful leader had made its impression.

Ambrosius forced himself into the gap between the two groups, and found a spot to stand on two shields. It was clear that the sight of their chief's head displayed before them had unsettled the Saxons and prompted a temporary halt to the fighting.

"Saxons! Your fight is over!" Ambrosius shouted, breaking the eerie silence.

"We have his sons as captives," he said, pointing to Hengist's head. "They are unhurt, and I gave my oath to your dying chief that they will be given the chance, as you all will, to leave this land. Throw down your weapons and submit!"

There was brief consultation amongst the Saxons and one man stepped forward.

"I am Ella, nephew of mighty Hengist, slain chief of the Saxons, whose head you now display before us. His dream of conquering this land lies dead with him. I can see with my own eyes that we are few and you are many. We shall hold you to your word, King of the Britons." He threw down his bloody axe and indicated to his men to do the same, although quietly seething with unsated rage.

"Thank God it is over," Brian said, voicing Ambrosius's thoughts.

13. The King's Return

DOGS SNAPPED AND bullied smaller ones as they squabbled over discarded offal, thrown out by a serving girl in the courtyard of The Miller tavern in Caer Gloui. The wild waters of the River Severn rushed below a green bank as revellers made the most of a warm sunny afternoon to sit outside on stools, watching the churning waters and scrapping dogs at their heels as they talked.

A drunken fight broke out, and soon two youths, swinging punches at each other, edged towards a table of elderly men. In a deceptively swift movement, the two young brawlers were grabbed from behind in a perfectly executed pincer attack by two grey-haired elders.

"Get your hands off me!" one of them cried.

"If there's any fighting to be done in my tavern, then I'll do it," Tomos growled in his ear. It was a voice that commanded respect. Tomos pushed the man away, and Brian released his opponent.

"Get out, the pair of you!" Tomos said, firmly planting his sandaled feet apart in readiness for any comeback. The young men scowled but, having taken in the build of the two retired soldiers, decided it best to leave.

"Anyway, where were we?" Tomos said, as the two brawny men returned to their stools.

"About to order more mead," said the balding third man, with a gap-toothed grin.

Brian laughed and signalled to the serving girl to come over. "Bring us mead and tell your mistress to send us meat and bread dipped in vinegar!"

"You could drink this alehouse dry, my friend," Tomos said with a rough smile, cracking the scar that ran down the left cheek of his sunburnt face. "Yes, you asked me about the Battle of Maisbeli, some twenty years past. It is true that I lay unconscious in the mud beneath a pile of bodies until my old legion mate, Bagdemagus, found me and hauled me to my feet. Our dear king, Ambrosius, was mighty relieved to see me alive, having ordered the entire battlefield be searched for my remains."

Brian nodded and said, "Aye, those of us who survived that merry slaughter were busy hauling the dead onto carts for hours afterwards. Over three thousand dead and half as many injured in an afternoon of bitter fighting. The Saxons would not yield until the few remaining were surrounded and could see the head of their chief, Hengist, displayed before them on a pole."

"It is an impressive story, although I have heard it many times," Drustan said, grinning as he rubbed his white stubble. "Our battle with the Jutes on the south coast was a chase, one skirmish after another. But we finally evicted them from the Isle of Vectis. Their feet were well planted, their settlement built. We took the locals who had fled to the mainland back there to occupy it and charged them with the defence of it."

Just then a breathless matron appeared, flanked by two serving girls, carrying platters of food.

"Do you old soldiers never tire of talking about wars and killing?" she said, sliding a platter of carved meat onto the table.

"Thanks, my love," said Tomos, pulling her onto his lap, "and you remembered to cut the pieces up small, so those of us with few teeth remaining can enjoy a nibble!"

Brian laughed, "I swear, you two look no different from that day you met in Calleva, when Regan was then the young serving maid!"

Regan beamed and rubbed Tomos's stubbly hair. "Now remember, do not get too drunk, you knights of the bear and whatever, we are all invited to the banquet tomorrow, over in

Corinium, to celebrate the king's return from Gaul." She pushed herself to her feet and then bustled away to the kitchen.

THE KITCHEN STAFF in Corinium were busy all day, preparing food and making sure there were enough barrels of mead and wine for the feast that night. Queen Gwendolyn would frequently appear in the doorway to ensure preparations were in hand.

"Stop shirking, you Saxon scum!" the portly Julius would shout as soon as she appeared, kicking the nearest unfortunate slave. One such was a surly, sulking fellow named Eopa. Since his arrival, some few months earlier, he had commanded the silent respect of the other slaves, over whom he seemed to have seniority. Julius now passed his instructions for them through Eopa, who spoke and understood his Brythonic tongue well enough, and would then delegate and organise.

"I have worked in the kitchens of lords before, sir," he had said on his arrival, feigning respect to the fat chief cook.

"Then show me how you would prepare a feast fit for a king," Julius had challenged him. To his annoyance, the ruse intended to embarrass the scruffy Saxon had backfired. Eopa produced the most delicious sauces and marinades, and made changes to the way they roasted and cured meat, drawing praise from the royal guests.

The fawning Julius was happy to take the credit, although by doing so had to agree to greater freedoms for Eopa to walk about the palace and go to the woods to pick herbs and mushrooms, and to dig for truffles. From that time, Eopa's influence grew, and he was now the chief sauce and soup maker, giving instructions to both slaves and free men alike.

Queen Gwendolyn knew his name, much to Julius's chagrin. "Eopa! The king has returned from his travels in Gaul, and I want you to surprise him with your special herb and mushroom soup."

"Yes, my lady," he replied, managing a half-bow, keeping his eyes on the aging queen in an almost insolent fashion.

Ambrosius, now in his sixtieth year, looked weary as he allowed his squire to undress him.

"A warm bath will ease your aching bones," Gwendolyn said, fussing over her husband. They now had three growing sons, the eldest of whom, David, had accompanied his father on his mission to aid King Constans in fighting Clovis, the latest king of the Franks. He was learning the duties of squire from his father's close attendant and former squire, Gawain, now a proven warrior.

"We have only delayed the inevitable, I fear," a weary Ambrosius said, wincing in pain as his leather jerkin was pulled over his head. "It is only a matter of time before the Franks sweep away the last remnants of the Roman Empire in the west. Eventually, my brother Constans will have to sue for peace."

Gwendolyn bustled around him, less concerned with politics and more with his scars and bruises. "This one is new," she said, touching a long, raised scar from a slashing blade.

"Ouch! That one is still sore, my love!" he said, pulling away from her delicate touch. "If it wasn't for Excalibur I would surely be dead. I am convinced that sword has magical powers that protect its bearer. There were times when it seemed to wield itself."

Gwendolyn held his crucifix and said, "It is our Lord God above who protects you, dear husband, not pagan magic." He smiled and kissed her forehead.

"After bathing with my essence of lavender oil, you can rest, my love, until the guests arrive for your feast. All your knights will be there, and those nobles living within easy reach. In summer, the roads are more tolerable and even Lupus, the old bishop, is expected. I must return to the kitchen." She swept out with her attendants, leaving Ambrosius to ease himself gently into his personal Roman bath, the luxury that reminded him of his youth, small in scale though it was. He waved the young maids away and beckoned to a fresh-faced youth to come and wash him.

It was an energetic blast of trumpets that later heralded the entrance of King Ambrosius and Queen Gwendolyn, who had donned ceremonial finery to celebrate the king's safe return. Silken cloaks, dyed in violet and blue and sewn with an accumulation of precious gems, glowed beneath gold crowns studded with polished diamonds and rubies, powerful symbols of protection. Behind them processed their three strong sons and attendants. Their two hundred guests, sitting at two long trestle tables, stood up and applauded. Ambrosius was indeed the Divine One; his longevity and success in battle, and the twenty years of relative peace in his kingdom, had already cemented his name as a great and invincible ruler.

Ambrosius remained standing and waited until the applause died down. He cast his steel-blue gaze over the assembled nobles and knights of his realm, noting the fine young men who had the looks of their departed fathers.

"My loyal subjects," he began, "I welcome you all to my hall to mark the occasion of my return to you from my visit to Amorica to my dear brother, King Constans. He sends you his greetings and wishes for peace in our kingdom of Britannia."

Sporadic applause broke out, and Ambrosius smiled benevolently before continuing. "I am pleased for the willing assistance you have rendered to my dear brother, Prince Uther, in fighting fresh waves of Angle and Saxon invaders in the east, and the Scotti and Picts to our north. I fear this will never end, as our pleasant land and plump farmsteads attract them like a corpse attracts flies."

Ambrosius grinned and nodded to encourage their laughter. "Also, I am pleased to hear reports that the son of Hengist, Octa, and his cousin, Ella, remain true to their word and kept the peace in the far north of our kingdom, providing a wedge between us and the unruly Picts and Votadani who swarm like angry bees over Hadrian 's Wall. This island took the mighty Julius Caesar, and those who followed him, two hundred years to tame, and I am aware that many of you have ancestors who fought against Roman dominion. But the idea of a united Britannia, with one ruling authority, came from the Romans, and I am sure you all now see the benefits of peace to reap your harvests and engage tradesmen in honest labour."

They banged their mugs on the table and grunted their agreement. Some dark looks were exchanged, noticed by Ambrosius, which served as a reminder that some had been disposed of lands to the Saxons, whilst others harboured thoughts of revenge for age-old grievances with neighbours or simply coveted others' lands. It was his position as high king that barely held together this loose alliance of tribal kings and chiefs. Also, his policy of appeasement to the Saxons after their defeat at Maisbeli was not universally welcomed.

"I see the faces of six of my original Knights of the Bear and Dragon, and am reminded that the appointment of new knights is overdue."

Fists hammered on the tables, causing the pewter plates, wine goblets and beakers to dance. Many in the room were hoping for recognition and higher status.

Eopa, standing in the doorway to the kitchen, had let out a low, rumbling laugh at the mention of obedient Saxon chiefs. Merlin's hand on his shoulder startled him.

"What are you doing listening to our king's speech, you wretch?" he demanded.

"Oh, erm, just on my way back to the kitchen, Master Merlin," he mumbled, "and stopped to listen to his wise words."

"His words are meant for his court, and not the likes of you! Begone!" Merlin watched him scurry back to the kitchens. It was he who had accompanied Eopa on his trips to the woods, noting the herbs and fungi he was gathering. But he also collected herbs and plants for his own healing concoctions, which meant he could not watch the sly devil all the time. So far, the slave's skills had only improved the meals he prepared.

Ambrosius drank some sweet wine before continuing. "Let us honour our knights with a toast. Arise Sirs Brian, Tomos, Tristan, Cadeyrn, Percival and Kay! And I must mention a seventh knight who has succeeded his noble uncle Triphun, and is now King Owain of Dyfed!"

Chairs were pushed back and the seven ageing warriors stood to a rousing reception. They were the heroes of the realm, having patrolled the borders of the kingdom in the high king's absence, fighting many a skirmish. At a signal from the king, platters of food then appeared from the kitchens to supplement the drink already in front of the rowdy guests.

Queen Gwendolyn beckoned a servant carrying a bowl of hot soup and whispered to Ambrosius, "Dear husband, I have had a special soup made in your honour; I hope you enjoy it."

Ambrosius smiled at her and kissed her rosy cheek. "My love, you have always thought of what pleases me."

Eopa stepped forward and served Ambrosius, ladling the thick mushroom soup into his bowl. Ambrosius glanced at him and nodded, indicating it was enough. Eopa withdrew as Ambrosius picked up his silver spoon.

"Who is that strange-looking fellow?" he asked Gwendolyn, affecting mild curiosity.

"That is Eopa, a Saxon slave who has brought knowledge of herbs and prepares delicious meals in our kitchen. Please try it, and tell me if it has the flavour of food you have tasted in Gaul."

Ambrosius dipped his spoon into the green broth and raised it to his lips, sucking in a mouthful and savouring the taste. His queen's endorsement of the Saxon was good enough for him to wave away the nagging suggestion in his mind that he should have it tasted. After all, his father was poisoned at the table...

"Mmmm, indeed it is good!" he said, smacking his lips.

The queen turned to her son, speaking with him on a light matter, as befitted the occasion, and Ambrosius continued to consume the broth. The room was full of talk and laughter as the nobility of the land tore into spit-roasted deer, boar and ox, and platters of cooked vegetables and flat bread.

To Ambrosius, who had set down his spoon, the sounds in the room became waves of noise that flowed in and out, like sea swell on a stony beach. Gwendolyn and Uther's worried faces floated before him as he pulled at the golden torque around his neck, as if it were strangling him.

"I cannot breathe!" he blurted out as he tried to stand, instead falling to his left, into the arms of Uther who held him up. The queen screamed as the room fell silent, and the last words Ambrosius heard before falling into unconsciousness was Uther shouting for the king's physician.

The table in front of him was cleared by Brian and Tomos, who laid out the convulsing king, both men alarmed at the sight of his frothing mouth.

Merlin appeared and attended to the dying man. He sniffed at the foam and then his eyes searched the table; bending forward, he spied an upturned soup bowl under it. He scanned the faces pressing in but could not see the one he hoped to find. Eopa was not there.

GWENDOLYN HAD LONG been in possession of the king's written instructions for the details of his funeral rites and had followed them devotedly. Pallbearers carried the body of Ambrosius shoulder high, along a dirt path through an ancient wood, past the reds of dogwood and cherry, stopping at a sacred lake, whose placid waters were guarded by green-leafed oaks bursting with birdsong.

The ancients believed a water goddess lived in the lake, and it was tradition to make an offering to her on the death of a leader, in the hope of a peaceful afterlife. Some warriors, chiefs and kings had wished their sword thrown into the water, prior to burial in mounds on sacred hills.

Christian priests trailed behind, silently assenting to the burial procession led by Merlin and the Druids. Their time would come to offer up a Christian blessing on the death of a great warrior-king who had championed the spread of Christianity throughout the land. They would offer their own words of comfort and eternal reward.

A Druid named Melchior took Excalibur from Uther and held the powerful blade aloft, speaking some words of reverence to the water goddess in Brythonic before hurling it through the air. The sun glinted off its polished blade, dazzling the eyes of the mourners. Merlin stood by, arms around the youngest son of Ambrosius, watching keenly from under his grey-cowled hood. He memorised the spot where the sword entered the water, counting the ripples until they reached the shore.

The funeral procession moved off, led by Druids before the pallbearers; the bier, escorted by tribal chiefs in shining armour and family members carrying their banners, was followed by chanting monks, making an odd but somehow appropriate union of pagan ritual and Christian belief. Merlin remained behind, until the lake waters had calmed and the goddess was still, walking slowly to the spot from where Excalibur had been thrown.

He picked up a heavy stone, weighing it in his hand before throwing it, counting the ripples as they came to his feet. Checking no one was about, he slipped off his woollen garment and entered the water, swimming steadily outwards until he was satisfied, and then dived beneath the surface. Would the water goddess approve? He felt a strong sense of duty to the unseen future of this land, a strong sense of destiny. Groping in the mud and twigs at the bottom, he found it.

UTHER WAS MADE king, as was his brother's wish. Part of the settlement was that Ambrosius's eldest son, David, would be recognised as heir apparent and reside with the queen at Corinium. The neighbouring cities of Caer Gloui and Caer Badon were each given to the two remaining sons to rule over. Uther grunted and kept his thoughts to himself at the coronation. He knew he would have to make a new seat of power, away from the cluster of these three Romano-Briton cities, linked so closely to his dead brother's family. He cared not for such detail, as Bishop Andreus of Gloui placed the crown on his head, and the chiefs and knights of the land bowed to him and one-by-one kissed his gloved hand.

He turned to his left and smiled at his daughter, Morgana, and next to her his sister Esther and brother-in-law Brian, his only surviving family. His wife Jessica had passed on some years earlier and he remained stubbornly unmarried. A new age beckoned, and Ambrosius had put in place the perfect system of government and military control. His new order of knights would be of the dragon, as the bear was buried with his brother, although somehow he felt that he was not finished with Artorus, the bear of myth and legend.

Merlin hovered close by, eager to remain in Uther's favour. A change in king could spark a civil war, but the brooding, hanging tension in the room soon dissipated as Uther spoke of peace and unity, and then made all the chiefs and knights swear an oath of loyalty to him. They knew him as a strong and powerful warrior and successful military leader, victor on the battlefield many times and the slayer of mighty Saxon chief, Horsa. They knew the politics of the court, and that if Ambrosius had not named him as his successor, Uther would no doubt have seized the crown and disposed of the children, who were too young to oppose their mighty uncle. They all knew that he was the best choice for a strong high king to unite the tribes in times of war and to keep the edgy peace that was constantly under threat.

Ambrosius Aurelianus, the Divine One, the last of the Romans, was dead, and Uther Pendragon was now their king.

Author's Note

Little detail remains of what happened in Britain in the fifth century following the departure of the Romans between AD 409 and AD 410, with perhaps the most reliable source being the historian, Gildas, whose bleak account of these troubled times dates from the early sixth century. He mentions only two leaders by name, "proud tyrant" Gurthigern (Vortigern to others) and Ambrosius Aurelianus. Other historians, including Bede the Venerable and Geoffrey of Monmouth, recount that Ambrosius defeats Vortigern and becomes King of Britannia. Bede describes him thus: "[He was] the sole member of the Roman race who had survived this storm in which his parents, who bore a royal and famous name, had perished. Under his leadership, the Britons regained their strength, challenged their victors to battle, and, with God's help, won the day."

In Gildas's history we see him as "...a gentleman who, perhaps alone of the Romans, had survived the shock of this notable storm. Certainly his parents, who had worn the purple, were slain in it... Under him our people regained their strength, and challenged the victors to battle. The Lord assented, and the battle went their way."

Ambrosius is credited by some historians with defeating Vortigern's army at the Battle of Gulloph, thought to be in the Wallops in Hampshire. Some years later, he further cemented his dominance by defeating a Saxon army at the Battle of Maisbeli, somewhere in South Yorkshire. Firm historical evidence is lacking for the exact locations and dates of these pivotal battles in early British history. Clearly, though, the Britons were fighting back, as another notable win against the

Saxons is mentioned at the Battle of Badon Hill, but which leader, the date and the location is obscured in the mist hanging over this beguiling period in our history.

With little else to go on, the life and accomplishments of Ambrosius Aurelianus remain in the shadowy realm of part-legend and part-history. This is, therefore, ideal territory for historical fiction, where the bones of the few surviving accounts of the period can be picked over and around which a story can be spun.

For more information on the author:
Website: http://timwalkerwrites.co.uk
Facebook: http://facebook.com/timwalkerwrites
Author Central: http://Author.to/TimWalkerWrites
Twitter: http://twitter.com/timwalker1666

Abandoned! – **Part One of** *A Light in the Dark Ages.*

Available to download now in e-book format from Amazon Kindle.

http://amazon.com/dp/B019D64AH0
http://amazon.co.uk/dp/B019D64AH0

Coming soon... *Uther's Destiny – A Light in the Dark Ages* part three.

18306960R00123

Printed in Poland
by Amazon Fulfillment
Poland Sp. z o.o., Wrocław